# Kingdom of the Elephants

# Kingdom o:

# he Elephants

ALAN C. JENKINS

ILLUSTRATED BY VICTOR G. AMBRUS

COVER PAINTING BY ROBERT J. LEE

FOLLETT PUBLISHING COMPANY
CHICAGO     NEW YORK

LIBRARY OF CONGRESS CATALOG CARD NUMBER:66-13713

*Copyright © 1963 Alan C. Jenkins. First published 1963 by Blackie &
Son Ltd., 5 Fitzhardinge Street, London, W.1., 17 Stanhope Street, Glasgow
Blackie & Son (India) Ltd., Bombay*

FIRST PRINTING

*To Nan, with Love*

# Author's Note

*Although I have always been interested in wild animals and can visualize no more exciting prospect than to live in some region where they are my constant neighbors, I had no intention of making them even one of my reasons for visiting India recently.*

*However, as I made my long journey through the southern states of Mysore, Coorg, Kerala and Madras, circumstances brought them more and more to my attention, particularly elephants. Everywhere I went, it seemed, they were dogging my footsteps; indeed, in some places, such as the famous High Range, they often literally barred my way. Staying among the tea gardens there, few days or nights passed without some elephantine disturbance or scandal, and the planters were full of tales and incidents about elephants.*

*But my main experience with elephants was in Coorg, now part of Mysore State. I stayed in forestry camps where elephants were both caught and tamed. I have never passed such a pleasant, fascinating and exciting time as then with the little Coruba tribesmen and the elephants for whom they had such a fondness and respect, feelings which this largest and noblest of land mammals inevitably evokes.*

*For the sake of atmosphere I have used occasional Indian words, Hindi or Tamil, and I hope my transliterations are not too inaccurate. I have not added a glossary, as any such words are explained in the context in which they are found.*

A.C.J.

# Kingdom of the Elephants

# 1

*The cracked bell*

They were so soft-footed they could not be heard. The gray dust of the jungle track rose so thickly they could not be seen. Yet the six camp elephants, marching back from work, together weighed more than twenty tons. They made less noise than a sambar deer as they hove majestically along in single file between the groves of feathery bamboo and the brilliant flame-of-the-forest trees. They made far less noise than a man in boots would, not that such a sight was to be seen for many miles around, unless you counted the canvas shoes of Ganesha Rao, the forestry officer.

Only the bells at the massive throats of the elephants jingled a refrain. Those bells might have sounded alike to a stranger, but every bell had a different note, some high, some solemn, some slow and lazy, and in the morning when the mahouts fetched the elephants from the jungle, where they had been turned out to browse, they could tell a mile away where each individual animal was. Anyone could tell where Rajendra was, for his bell was cracked and rang with a tuneless note. Some of the mahouts said he had cracked his bell on purpose, so that its sound would not carry so far, and it would take all the longer to trace him.

Now the elephants had come into the pulsing sunshine again, and their huge bodies loomed up murkily through the churning dust. Trunks dangling, tusks glinting, sleepy eyes blinking, they plodded on, while high up on their colossal backs the mahouts squatted. On they marched, with humping shoulders, down through a long deep ravine in which the grass grew taller than a man and in fact hid the camp attendants who were following the elephants. Only by a white *puggaree* here or a gleaming face there could one have seen that Tumbi and Gopal and the rest were padding through the dust alongside the elephants.

The jungle watched them pass, elephants and men. In the stinkwood trees black-faced monkeys sat and stared as they scratched for fleas. Then, as if to spread the news of the elephant procession, though they saw it frequently, they went whooping and bounding away, swinging from branch to branch with crazy skill. Golden orioles plunged through the trees like shafts of light. Tiny green bee-eaters darted out after insects. A racket-tailed drongo looked around for someone to pester. Somewhere a copper-smith bird began beating out his monotonous tune of *tonk tonk tonk*, to show he could do better than the elephant bells. In a sudden shattering frenzy of noise, the cicadas opened up their metallic, sizzling chorus, which was like the cry of the tortured earth panting under the sun.

While the other camp attendants lagged behind, Tumbi hurried to keep up with the fast-striding elephants who were impatient for the evening bath and, even more so, for the evening ration of rice and jaggery. Naked except for his white *dhoti*, which he had tucked round his waist and between his legs like a loincloth, he ran silently parallel to the file of great animals.

However many times Tumbi saw the elephants, his wonder was never dulled. He was with them all day long, during their intermittent workdays or when the wild elephants were captured or put through their training. He was never far away from them at any hour of the day, for Munjara was the kingdom of the elephants. In the training camp or in the vastness of the surrounding jungle, the elephants reigned. As the royal presence is felt at all times in a palace even where the king might be unseen by many of his servitors, so did the presence of the elephants dominate the countryside of Munjara.

Tumbi watched the elephants now as he loped on between the clusters of bamboo. Assuredly there was nothing so marvelous, so splendid, as the elephants. It was no wonder that one of the Hindu gods took the form of an elephant. No wonder that in many temples hundreds of carved elephants symbolically bore up the walls on their backs. Yet it was strange that though the elephants were so vast and strong and powerful, they could also be so wise and gentle. It was strange, too, that they alone of all the animals, lived to the same age as men.

Tumbi's eyes grew wide every time he looked at those gigantic bodies, those great columns of legs, that padded along silent as shadows on the cushioned feet. His nostrils flared with excitement when he saw them gather up a heavy log in their trunks and toss it down like a plaything. Yet those same trunks could delicately pick up a berry like a man using finger and thumb. Or again, how awe-inspiring it was when perhaps Rajendra and Krishna manhandled a big tusker caught in one of the pit traps in the jungle. When those great bodies clashed and struggled it was like some echo from another world, a world dominated by the animals instead of men.

Yet these forest giants, who were endowed with a terrible primeval force, would obey the slightest word of a puny man.

While the dusty file ambled past through the ravine, Tumbi darted on in company, glancing up enviously at the mahouts who lorded it high up there, nonchalantly dangling their brown slim legs behind the huge, idly flapping ears. One day he himself would be sitting up on one of the elephants, as by rights he should be by now, for few men knew more about elephants than he did. He had scarcely been able to walk when he was venturing under the legs of the great bulls or being picked up in their trunks and placed proudly on their backs. He had learned much from his father of these elephants.

Occasionally he stole a ride on Rajendra, biggest and oldest and most skillful of the tuskers, when he could get out in the jungle any morning before Kalyan went in search of his mount. Sometimes he rode the young captives after they had been broken in, but they were sent away to other camps, and he never

15

really got to know them long enough. Tumbi eyed the gray hairs of Kalyan's head. One day the chief mahout would no longer be able to work, for it was a hard, racking life for those who served the elephants. That would be Tumbi's chance, even though Gokul and Gopal and some of the other camp attendants were older than he was. But he hoped Rajendra would still be fit for work even when Kalyan no longer rode him.

Now Rajendra, striding ever more eagerly, was leading the way into the camp. At the head of the ravine, the jungle had abruptly ended and here was nothing but flat beaten earth and a few big trees for shade. Tumbi pattered close alongside Rajendra who towered above him, never-ending. If you looked up at the high domed wise-looking forehead, it was enough to give you a crick in the neck.

Fearlessly Tumbi placed a hand on the rough, age-old, wrinkled skin as Rajendra strode on, and the old elephant gently curled his pink-faced trunk and touched him on the shoulder. But Kalyan kicked the elephant on the neck with his naked heel and made him turn away from the boy.

"Out of the way, little frog," the mahout teased from on high; "else thou wilt be trampled on when the mighty pass by."

"Thou art all wind, old gray head," Tumbi re-

torted, cheerfully; "if thou didst not hang on with thine ankus, thou wouldst assuredly float off like a cloud into the sky."

"Take thyself off," jeered Tipane, the second mahout, who was riding Krishna. "The elephants will think thee a white ant and be afraid thou wilt get into their trunks and drive them mad!"

"Thou art like a cattle egret on the back of a water buffalo!" yelled Tumbi, his dark eyes dancing, for there was nothing like a bit of repartee to add spice to the day. "And thy cackle is like the noise of a jungle cock!"

"Take care the mongoose does not hear *thee* cackling," shouted Govindra from Tilly's back; "or he will think there are eggs to be stolen!"

All the mahouts had something to say to Tumbi, but he had an answer for them all in return. He was safe in the knowledge that his dead father had been acknowledged supreme among mahouts. Tumbi's father had even been appointed mahout to the Maharajah, and at the glittering Dasara festival, he used to ride the sacred elephant who was saddled with a howdah so superbly decorated and bedizened that it took more than a score of men to lift it on to the animal's back. That howdah was so heavy that three months before the festival the elephant was put on a special diet to give him sufficient strength for his task.

Though some folk said it was also because the Maharajah weighed so much, too. The Maharajah had presented the elephant's bell to Tumbi's father who in turn had left it to Tumbi when he died. It was the only thing he had to leave his son, but Tumbi treasured it as if it had been wrought of gold instead of brass. One day he would hang that fine brass bell on Rajendra's neck instead of the cracked one that now rang so dolefully as the elephants made their way through the camp.

Near the huge teakwood cages in which the wild elephants were imprisoned when they were first brought home from the jungle pit traps, the mahouts made the camp elephants kneel down, with legs stretched out before and behind. Then their back-pads and harness were removed, their legs and feet carefully examined for signs of chafing or thorns, and, the mahouts now on foot, the elephants ambled down to the nearby lake beyond the thatched huts for their bath and scrub.

"Hold back, then!" Kalyan reproached Rajendra, who went storming off eagerly. "Thou art like a jackal that smells carrion from afar off!" For he knew that Rajendra wanted to have done with his bath and get down to the serious business of supper. With ponderous delight, the elephants waded out into the cool water, welcome after the steamy heat of the day. Trumpeting joyously, they disappeared until nothing but gray backs and huge domed heads showed as they wallowed there. They filled their trunks and squirted refreshing draughts of water into their mouths. They squirted each other with mud and water. Krishna and Pundit started a barging match. Each wrapped his trunk round the other's, then they braced their legs and pulled and pushed in amiable jostling. The elephants knew their strength and were careful not to injure each other. Tilly waded out and nudged Krishna in the backside as if to tell him not to go too far.

Now, at a word, the elephants sank down on their sides while Tumbi and Gopal and Gokul scrubbed them and scrubbed them again with great forest burrs amid a cheerful babble of talk. Those who had to do with elephants were always cheerful. Ganesha Rao had ordered that Krishna's tusks should be tipped. While Tumbi lashed the elephant's trunk to one leg to keep it from being cut, Tipane sawed away at the thick ivory. Every now and then he dipped the saw in the water to prevent it getting hot. Krishna wallowed on his mountainous side and blinked his eyes. Leaning on that gigantic back, Tumbi marveled that this huge animal should submit so docilely. Surely it could only be because the elephant was wise and could understand that it was for his own good or rather perhaps for the good of the other elephants. Blunt tusks could do less harm than those sharp as a sword.

Like a great wave, the water of the lake swirled as the elephants heaved themselves up again, gleaming from their scrub and refreshed by their drink. The sun had gone down behind the jungle. In the trees the fruit bats were beginning to rustle. The fires were twinkling brightly among the thatched huts. Away in the distance, the jackals were shrieking like lost souls. Soon the darkness of the tropical night would descend like the fringe of a soft thick curtain.

Back to the camp, the elephants strode, trumpeting now for their food. Many a man got worse food than the elephants did. Many a family would have been unable to eat so much. Thirty pounds of boiled rice mixed with sweet jaggery sugar, each elephant received every day.

"I will feed Rajendra for thee," Tumbi offered to Kalyan and the old mahout grunted agreement, for he was weary and anxious to get on with his own meal.

"But see then thou givest all to the elephant and dost not cram thine own belly with jaggery!" he chided, as he limped away to the huts.

Tumbi was content as he stood there, dwarfed by the placid old bull.

"Hai! Thou hast a great belly to fill, old father!" He grinned as he popped lumps of food into the elephant's mouth. In Mysore, his father had often told him contemptuously, the mahouts threw the food on the ground for the elephants to pick up. That was wrong. An elephant deserved more respect than that, and his food should be handed to him deferentially.

"Is there no end to that elephant's greed?" demanded Gopal, who was feeding Tilly. "That one receives more food than all the camp together!"

"Is he not the mightiest and the finest of all the elephants?" retorted Tumbi, popping another lump into Rajendra's ever-ready maw. By way of appreciation, the old elephant's belly rumbled as he champed away at the good food.

At last even Rajendra had had his fill or, rather, inquiringly nuzzling Tumbi with the tip of his trunk, he resigned himself to the fact that there was no more. Now all the camp elephants were hobbled with a length of chain round one leg, for they were allowed to wander off into the jungle at night to stuff themselves with succulent bamboo leaves and other fodder. Their cooked food was good, but they still required many hundreds of pounds of green stuff to sustain them. Ganesha Rao once said that a full-grown elephant ate the weight of more than four men in jungle food every day. He would despoil five acres of the jungle in satisfying his hunger.

"*Salaam!*" cried Tumbi, when he had put the padded leg chain on Rajendra, and the elephant raised his curled trunk on high and trumpeted a salute in reply.

"*Salaam!*" cried Gopal to Tilly.

"*Salaam!*" cried Gokul to Krishna and in turn each of the camp elephants saluted in response at the end of another day. The trees rang with the sound. As if to point out that they had been created by the same power that created the mighty elephants, the mosquitoes sounded out their own minute shrill cry.

As the elephants trudged away into the stirring jungle, with jingling bells and clanking chains, Tumbi himself felt hungry. He squatted in the camp longhouse with the mahouts and the attendants, flicking the rice into his mouth with deft fingers, and while he ate, he listened to the fading sound of Rajendra's cracked bell. One day he would hang a better bell round that great, gray, wrinkled neck.

# 2

*The Great King appears*

Tumbi was in the deep jungle of Munjara. He had gone there in company with Bapundi the tracker who knew the ways of the elephants better than other men knew the ways of their water buffalo or their milch cow. He could read the wind better than he could read a book. In fact, like Tumbi, he could not read, and when he signed his name, he did so with a thumb print. But he could tell a story from a crushed blade of grass or a scratch on the bark of a tree. He could tell the difference between the tracks of a wild pig and a young sambar, which not all men could do. He knew that an animal which ran down its quarry had bigger toes than had an animal which stalked its prey. He used the words of men very little, and it would never have surprised Tumbi to hear him speak some language known only to the creatures of the forest. Bapundi had no home. If he needed shelter in the jungle, he simply cut out the middle stems of a bamboo tree, and he had an excellent hut for his pains. For food, he depended on wild fruit and succulent roots and honey from the nests of wild bees. He was expert with a two-stringed bow and mud pellets and sometimes hunted the flying cats and other creatures, for Bapundi would eat meat when it came his way like some men of low caste.

Tumbi went off with Bapundi as often as he could, for he knew that where the tracker was there the wild elephants of Munjara would be also, even if that meant traipsing many miles after them. Now Tumbi and Bapundi squatted still as chunks of wood near the great river that flowed through the jungle. Everywhere was slashed with color. Snake birds with sinuous necks sat on dead trees waiting to dart after fish. A flock of scarlet minivets went hovering and fluttering through the trees. A paradise flycatcher trailed his long tail ribbons in a loop as he went twisting nimbly after insects. As brilliant as the birds were the red flower cups of the tulip trees, the waxy petals of the coral tree. Huge swallow-tailed butterflies, with wings as wide as the span of a man's hand, flitted and tilted from flower to flower, sipping the nectar.

But Tumbi had no eyes for all this loveliness. He was right: where Bapundi was there the elephants would be, too! Down in the river, a family of them were bathing. There was the mother and her two sons of different ages and a cow elephant that kept her company. The elder of the two young elephants was a few years old; the other one was only about eighteen months.

All the elephants were enjoying their bath. The two grown-ups and the elder son solemnly squirted water over themselves and each other, but the baby of the family had found a very satisfying pool of liquid mud near the bank. He kept sucking this up in his trunk and depositing a mud pie on his head. He was beginning to acquire quite a crown of mud. Sometimes he varied this by squirting a trunkful of mud at his mother's back and once his brother rebuked him for this disrespectful attitude by squirting water back at him, at which the young elephant squealed in delight.

Tumbi put his hand to his mouth. Even Bapundi's eyes danced at it all. But the slightest movement would have alarmed the elephants; as it was, something was making the cow elephant uneasy. She stood in the swirling water, trunk questing, one foot raised irresolutely, a hind leg stretched out, big ears twitching.

The other cow was restless, too.

Something was happening in the jungle. Farther away among the trees and the tall yellow grass, the rest of the herd was tramping about uneasily. They had finished their bathing beforehand, and now Tumbi could hear them tearing down branches. Even when you could not see the elephants, the very sound of their ravaging made you glance about you for a way to run.

Presently the mother elephant decided to join the herd. She and the other cow strode out of the river, shepherding the two young ones with them. But the young baby did not want to quit his mud pies. It was all too much fun. While the other three marched on up into the jungle, he seized the first opportunity of slipping back and gleefully started to squirt mud over himself again.

Tumbi's white teeth flashed in a sudden grin against his dark face. There was going to be trouble. Bapundi sucked in his breath.

It was not long before the mother elephant realized her baby was not with her. She came striding back down to the river and without any further ado made straight for her erring son. She gave him a resounding slap with her trunk that rang out across the river like the crack of a gun and made the young elephant squeal indignantly and scuttle away. This time the cow elephant made certain he did not sneak back to his game. Still crowned with his mud pie but with head bowed ruefully at such unkind treatment, he walked sedately by his mother's side.

Bapundi sniffed the breeze carefully and then, followed by Tumbi, cautiously made his way up into the jungle. There was no difficulty in keeping track of the elephants, for, apart from the devastation they left behind them, they were making so much noise. The family party had by now joined the rest of the herd, and they all seemed to be tramping to and fro as if they could not make up their minds what to do. Some of them were trumpeting loudly in an angry tone. Occasionally Tumbi caught a glimpse of a snaking trunk or an immense ear against the skyline.

He sniffed the air as carefully as Bapundi. He knew it was vital to know how the wind was blowing. Your life might depend on it. Especially now when he and Bapundi were so near the elephants. If the herd got wind of them, they would have to flee for their lives; for the elephants were in a dangerous mood and though the great beasts could not run, they could stride as fast as a galloping horse.

The thrashing of branches and tramping of great feet grew louder, and now Tumbi could see various huge bodies churning about in the shuddering trees. Long trunks snaked up and ripped down branches, not to eat but in anger. An elephant trumpeted, a furious, frightened squeal. The baby elephants huddled near their mothers. Even the one with the mud pie crown was very sober now. He knew there was danger about.

But it was not the presence of the men that had alarmed the elephants. There was only one thing that could be upsetting them like this and that was tiger. Somewhere in the jungle a tiger was skulking, hoping for a chance of attacking one of the baby elephants. Maybe he would not be able to kill it outright now, but if he could stampede the herd, he might be able to cripple the baby and finish it off later on.

Crouching in the tawny grass, Bapundi watched and listened. The evidence of the jungle flowed into his senses and was absorbed like ink in blotting paper. Behind him Tumbi waited tensely, holding one wrist in his other hand. He knew what had upset the elephants. He knew the jungle too well to have to ask Bapundi.

While the sunlight falling through the branches glinted on their naked limbs and backs, they crouched in the grass watching the elephants who one moment

29

stood facing in a certain direction and the next had wheeled round ponderously, trunks up questing the air, trying to locate the tiger.

They seemed leaderless. They did not know what to do. The herd consisted of cow elephants and half-grown bulls and a few babies. If only they could make certain where the tiger was hiding, they could act. But clearly the tiger was skirting the herd, exploring the possibilities of an attack then or later, working the elephants up into such a commotion that he would have more hope of success.

For more than an hour, the herd tramped to and fro on the slope above the river, while Bapundi and Tumbi shifted their ground accordingly, keeping a watchful eye open for the tiger as well as the elephants. Sometimes they were less than fifty yards from the herd, and Tumbi's heart beat a tune of mingled fear and excitement as he peered through the tall grass at the stamping, restless feet.

As they furtively kept pace with the elephants, they came across a flat open space where nothing grew, not even a blade of grass. It was a sambar's stamping-ground, trampled by many generations of deer. In the dust was unmistakable evidence of the tiger's presence.

Bapundi came to a halt and dropped on one knee alongside a set of pug marks. They were comparatively long and narrow to his expert eye. "Tigress," he said. That was all.

Tumbi stood very still and licked his lips. Hitherto they had only guessed at the tiger's presence. Now these pug marks, clearly defined in the fine dust of the sambar's ring, proved beyond doubt that she was there, somewhere, a striped killer moving more like silent water than muscle and bone and sinew.

All the jungle was on the alert now. In the distance, a muntjac deer barked a warning. Jungle fowl were calling in alarm. Even the racket-tailed drongos had ceased to pester the gray, grizzly jungle babblers who scratched among the dead leaves. Everyone knew that somewhere—but where?—a stealthy body was creeping, skulking, elusive as a shadow. Away through the groves of bamboo, a sounder of wild pig went scampering and grunting. They had been making their way down to the river when they scented the tiger. A huge old boar with great hairy muscled shoulders and curving tushes paused to test the air. He was afraid of nobody and would have given a good account of himself even with a tiger. All the same, he wanted to avoid trouble if possible.

Suddenly Tumbi felt Bapundi's hand on his arm. The wizened little tracker said no word, that would have been a waste of time, but Tumbi saw that he was looking at the skyline of the hill, and he turned his gaze there also. What he saw made him draw in his breath in astonishment and wonder.

"It is the Great King," he whispered, in an awed tone.

In a gap in the trees, silhouetted against the sky, a bull elephant had appeared. He was magnificent, bigger even than Rajendra. There was no mistaking his identity. This elephant was famous throughout Munjara. Both Bapundi and Tumbi knew him well by sight and by reputation. The Great King was Munjara.

"The Great King!" Even Bapundi echoed Tumbi's words and crouched lower as if making obeisance before this majestic creature.

The Great King was moving fast. Downhill he strode. The slope was steep, and he zigzagged his way along a track the herds had used for longer than any man knew.

But even this thundering stride was too slow for the great bull. He could tell that the herd was upset, that they desperately needed his leadership. He left the track and, incongruously tucking his mighty hind legs under him, slid down the rest of the slope on his rump, amid a cloud of dust and a crashing of foliage. Tumbi would have laughed at this sight, but the Great King was terrible in his anger. At the bottom

of the slope, he strode on through the jungle; and the earth trembled as he passed less than a stone's throw from the crouching figures in the grass.

Tumbi's breath came quickly. It was as if a mighty god had passed by.

Straight to the herd the Great King stormed. At once he began to knock some sense into them. He stamped around chivvying the cow elephants together, poking them with his tusks, lashing the young bulls with his trunk, trumpeting a rallying cry. It was as well not to be an enemy of the elephants at that moment.

Bapundi and Tumbi crept nearer to watch. But they took heed to watch the wind also.

Masterfully the Great King rounded up the herd, mustered them together in orderly fashion. A chorus of trumpeting startled the air. There was a new note of confidence in it. Now the herd was no longer uncertain. Their leader had returned. Now they would seek out the foe who had menaced their babies and deal with her as she deserved.

Led by the Great King, the elephants moved off briskly in single file through the jungle, the babies in the middle of the procession, the bigger animals at the head and tail of the line. Ears flapping and trunks questing, they strode off purposefully. Evidently they had got full wind of the tiger and woe betide her if she stayed in the path of the angry elephants.

Knowing they were safe while the herd con-
centrated on the tiger, Bapundi and Tumbi followed
eagerly in their tracks. It was as if a storm had swept
through the jungle. The undergrowth was trampled
flat, branches had been broken like twigs. Like one
immense live battering-ram, the elephants had bashed
their vengeful way onward.

For a long time, Bapundi and Tumbi followed
the herd which they could hear and see all the while,
milling and thrashing round, like beaters in a hunt.
Not for a moment did the furious trumpeting cease.
An elemental fury permeated the breathless jungle.

But the herd did not find the tigress. Even she
was chastened by this fury. She went while the going
was good, and Tumbi caught a glimpse of a furtive
striped shadow gliding away ignominiously deep
down the jungle near the river. The tigress had more
sense than to stay and argue things out with the angry
herd. The coming of the Great King had put an end
to her scheme.

The Great King was fearsome in his anger at
failing to run down the tigress. When at length he
knew that she had indeed escaped, his fury knew no
bounds. He thrashed the branches with his trunk,
picked up huge limbs of wood and hurled them here
and there at random. He roared with pent-up wrath,

and Tumbi shivered to hear it. Usually an elephant squeals or trumpets, but now the Great King roared until the trees rang.

Then he strode furiously towards a nearby tree. He pushed and pushed against it, bashed it and bashed it until it shook. Again and again and again, he attacked the tree until, with a snapping of roots and crashing of branches, he got it down. Even then, he was not satisfied. He went to work on that tree with his powerful tusks and ripped it up right and left while splinters of wood spattered from side to side.

Sweat broke from Tumbi's slender body as he witnessed this majestic fury. He felt almost glad that the tigress had escaped such a fate. The whites of his eyes flicked as he glanced at Bapundi. Now a deep, startling silence had fallen on the jungle as the Great King gradually calmed down. He stood there, suddenly alert, as if aware he was being watched. The folds of his ears, his sunken cheeks, revealed his great age but did not in the least detract from the grandeur of his presence. Truly, thought Tumbi, the Great King is lord of Munjara.

Bapundi touched Tumbi on the arm.

"We must go," his eyes said, though his tongue was silent.

Silent, too, were his naked feet as he led the way

back through the sheltering grass. Death might have been the penalty for an ill-placed step. One moved carefully in the presence of the Great King's displeasure.

# 3

*Pitfall*

Bapundi and Tumbi were on their way to visit
some of the tracker's pit traps in the jungle. The traps
had been dug on tracks the elephants used on their
way to their watering places or salt licks or special
bamboo groves where they knew they would find
good feeding. For many generations elephants had
used these tracks which were broad as a road and in
fact better than many a man-made road, worn smooth
and flat by the passing and repassing of giant bodies.
The wild elephants traveled many miles for their

food, they had their regular migrations, and sometimes did not visit a particular district for months.

But Bapundi always knew where they were, and in the catching season, he was always prepared. He renovated the traps as carefully as a man might tend his own house.

The elephants were wise in their ways. Bapundi had to be wiser. He had to outwit them, deceive them, lure them into the traps. The wild elephants had to be caught because there were not enough in captivity to breed from, and there was always more and more work to be done, more and more timber to be hauled to fill India's needs.

Bapundi used to tell Tumbi of the days when the *kheddah* took place, and then he would talk excitedly, spilling out more words in five minutes than he normally did in five years.

"Only once in seven years did the *kheddah* take place," he said, chewing the betel nut that stained his teeth and mouth a devilish red. "Then the great prince, the Maharajah, would hire thousands of men to beat the jungle. Scores of trained elephants would be ridden by the best mahouts . . ."

"My father among them," put in Tumbi, for he had heard about the *kheddah* many times.

"Ay, he was a man, thy father," said Bapundi. "He would lead the *kheddah*. Slowly, through many days and nights, the herd would be gathered together, drawn close in a noose until all were driven into the great stockade. Hai! Then it was a sight for brave men's eyes to see how the trained elephants, *our* elephants, warred against the wild ones and thrashed them into submission . . ."

Those indeed were great days, and Bapundi's eyes gleamed as he thought of all the thrill and danger and pride of capturing the whole herd in one spectacular operation. Now he had to be content with the jungle pit traps, and he spat out a stream of red juice as he squatted there talking elephant talk to Tumbi.

Nevertheless, Bapundi's traps were the work of a craftsman. Especially their coverings. Anyone could dig a trap (though it was hard work, and took a long time) with *mommetties* to scrape away the soil, which all had to be removed in heavy baskets carried on the heads of a string of men and women. But to cover a trap so that it would deceive those trunks that inspected every inch of the ground as the elephants marched through the jungle: that indeed could only be done by one who dwelt all his days in the jungle.

Even Tumbi could not discern Bapundi's traps, so cunningly were the covers made of branches and dead leaves and grass. None but Bapundi could tell that they were not part of the jungle floor. There were few creatures of the jungle that Bapundi could not deceive, and many besides elephants had suddenly found the ground opening beneath them as they crashed into the pit concealed by the network of leaves Bapundi had woven. Once a gaur—one of the huge wild oxen that men mistakenly call bison—was caught in a trap. To have shot it would have been simple, but Ganesha Rao decreed that it must be liberated. So it was, after much sweat and fear, and it charged and wounded Rajendra grievously in the process of being freed.

That day as Bapundi and Tumbi went barefoot and silent along one of the elephant roads, they could see plainly that several animals had passed that way recently; in fact during the night. All around was the trail of devastation that elephants always leave, for giants are untidy eaters. Here and there, too, were stupendous piles of dung and in one of them Bapundi stuck a toe.

"Cold but not cold." He nodded meditatively. "They came this way perhaps in the morning."

Yes, the herd had passed that way a few hours ago. Now already they were several miles away . . . all but one of them who had remained behind! A fine, half-grown bull, proud of his growing tusks, he had been playing roughly with a young cow, barging her on when she stopped to pluck some forest fruit. She

41

had moved out of his way and he had started to rip down branches of bamboo that drooped above the track. Good and succulent were those feathery leaves, and the young bull became absorbed in stuffing them into his mouth, wrenching them down with a dexterous twist of his trunk. Pace by pace he shuffled on until suddenly, with a half-eaten branch sticking out of his mouth, he went down on his knees as if his legs had been knocked from under him.

Desperately he struggled to recover, but his weight carried him forward, and he went crashing down amid a violent rustling of leaves and cracking of twigs, while the rest of the herd stampeded away, trumpeting shrilly in alarm and leaving the dazed young bull to flounder in Bapundi's pit.

Fortunately he was not hurt. Because of the elephants' huge size and weight, there was always a risk that they might be injured when they fell into a trap. Festooned with dead foliage, the young bull clambered to his feet. For a while, he stood there immobile in bewilderment. Then he felt his way about the pit with his questioning trunk, but it was evident that the pit was deep and there was no escape. An elephant cannot stride more than six feet, and Bapundi's trap was far too big for the young bull to get out of it, for his back did not even reach to the top of the walls.

Now the jungle was silent but for the *tonk tonk*

*tonk* of the coppersmith bird and the high-pitched cries of blossom-headed parakeets, for the herd had vanished like gray shadows after the first crashing stampede. Had the young bull been sick or hurt, they might have returned to help him. But he had simply disappeared inexplicably into the earth—and there he was, raging helplessly.

He was still blundering about the confines of the pit when Bapundi found him. By now he had recovered from his shock and was exceedingly angry at what had happened. He squealed and rushed at the side of the pit where the two half-naked humans stood regarding him.

"A good young bull," said Bapundi, appraisingly. "Sixteen years, maybe eighteen."

"He has spirit. He will make a good worker," said Tumbi, squatting down out of range of the trunk with its wet pink end. It was strange to think that this young captive was about the same age as himself. "One day he will take Rajendra's place."

Meanwhile, Bapundi circled the pit, surveying the young elephant with an expert eye for signs of any damage to its limbs. But he was soon satisfied, for the elephant was too active to have suffered any hurt. Bapundi was always better pleased when a younger animal was caught; not only was there less likelihood of its damaging itself as it fell, but also it was much

44

easier to get out of the pit and subsequently much more tractable in its training. Rarely was a full-grown elephant caught, occasionally a cow and her calf, but never a cunning old bull such as the Great King. He had survived three score years of hazards in the jungle. He knew all about Bapundi's traps.

"Now," said the tracker to Tumbi, glancing at the sun as he spoke, "thou must go thy fastest and inform *Peria Dorai*, Big Master, that we have an elephant for him. Two hours for thee to reach the camp, three for all to be made ready and the camp elephants to be brought here . . . Yea, we will get this bull into the stockade well before nightfall."

"*Serri!*" agreed Tumbi, jumping to his feet. "All right! I am gone! I go the river way as far as the mangrove swamp; thence along the old track and through the village."

This was a longer way round to the camp, but the short way led past a certain hole where it was well known that a king cobra, a hamadryad, deadliest and most aggressive of snakes, dwelt, and Tumbi had no intention of courting trouble for the sake of saving a couple of miles.

The morning mists had cleared, and necklaces of dew sparkled on leaf and stem as he loped through the jungle. The little jungle cocks crowed fussily as they skulked away. A sambar buck belled in alarm and went crashing through the undergrowth. A horn-bill cackled raucously. Dainty little green lorikeets awoke from roosting head downwards in the trees and began to tear at the petals of coral tree flowers, beauty destroying beauty.

All this Tumbi saw and yet did not see, as he hurried through the jungle that throbbed and teemed and flashed and shrieked with life. The sights and sounds of the wild were as natural to him as his own breathing, but he did not have to tell himself all the time that he was drawing breath.

He walked fast, eager to bear the news to Ganesha Rao. Where the shade was thicker, he some-times went at a jog trot, and the sweat glistened on his body. By the time he reached the rutted dirt road, the sun was striking down with fierce blows, gradu-ally stilling the jungle into the stupor of noontide.

In the village, spotted doves examined the road for grain. Contemplative rhesus monkeys sat at the foot of the tamarinds and watched the boy go past. Women in gay saris were returning from the well with brass chatties on their heads. The village cow-herd was driving the hump-backed cattle out to pasture, and Tumbi spat at their dust. Bullock carts creaked by, accompanied by a jingling of bells on the hubs of the wheels. In the paddy fields, an ugly old water buffalo hauled a plough behind which an old man staggered. A watchman was returning home from guarding the orange groves, whose fruit hung like bright lanterns on the trees. Pack donkeys laden with skinfuls of toddy trotted by.

"Where dost thou come from, and what is the news, Tumbi?" an old woman demanded, as she sat by the village stream pounding clothes against a stone.

"From the jungle!" answered Tumbi, not without a touch of pride. "We have caught a tusker, Bapundi and I!"

"One less to steal my plantains!" said the old woman. Round her house—and round many others in the neighborhood—was a deep wide trench to keep the wild elephants out.

Many people asked Tumbi what news he had; if they did not, he informed them all the same—and the news from the jungle did not lose in the telling.

However, when at length, rather wearily, he reported at the bungalow along the camp track, he gave a strictly accurate account to Ganesha Rao.

"*Salaam, iyer!*" he said, briefly putting the palms of his hands together in front of his face in salute. "There is an elephant in the trap north of the big river . . ."

"How old? Is it unharmed? A bull or a cow?" demanded Ganesha Rao, a tall man who wore khaki drill and a pith helmet.

"It is a bull, *Peria Dorai*," Tumbi told him. "It is unharmed and has been in the trap for a few hours. A big herd passed that way during the night. Yesterday we saw the Great King . . ."

"How old is the new bull?" repeated Ganesha Rao.

"Bapundi says, perhaps sixteen, perhaps eighteen years."

"*Serri*! All right!" The forestry officer nodded. "Thou hast done well. Tell the cook to give thee chapaties to eat. We must go straightaway."

He walked down the veranda steps and called a servant to send instructions to the elephant camp for Rajendra, Tilly, and Krishna to be got ready at once with ropes. He himself would drive in the jeep as far as the big river and then continue on foot. A peon rode off on a bicycle along the camp track to take the instructions.

Tumbi gathered all this as he sat in the kitchen regaling the cook with a story of the capture and himself with fresh-cooked chapaties and a slice of pawpaw fruit. At once he rushed out, almost choking with food.

"*Doringlee*! Master! May I come with you to the trap?" he asked, eagerly.

If he went on foot, he might be too late. For a moment, Ganesha Rao looked stern, and Tumbi was afraid he was angry at such an impudent request. But then he smiled gaily under his thick black moustache.

"Truly thou art the son of thy father, Tumbi," he said, approvingly. "The elephants are in thy blood . . . though thou art smaller than a mouse!" He laughed at his own joke and clambered into the jeep that stood waiting ready.

Tumbi laughed, too, stuffed the last chapati into his mouth and hopped into the jeep as well. He had never ridden in a car before, and he hung on with both hands as the vehicle went swaying and bouncing along the dusty camp road.

But he folded his arms as they came up to the waiting mahouts presently. It was on the tip of his tongue to yell out some pleasantry to the astonished Kalyan as the jeep drew to a standstill, but he decided that in Ganesha Rao's presence he had better keep quiet.

# 4

*Flight for freedom*

Rajendra marched through the jungle. He was half as old again as Tilly or Krishna, yet his step was brisk, and the younger elephants had to stride smartly to keep up with him.

The elephant bells jingled pleasantly and were echoed by the cries of the jungle babblers. Even Rajendra's cracked bell seemed to ring out boldly as the old elephant brushed aside creepers and branches, and Kalyan lay flat on his back for safety.

"Rajendra smells the jungle," thought Tumbi, as

he watched the old tusker approach. "Perhaps he remembers his youth!"

It was strange to think that nearly half a century had passed since Rajendra roamed free in the jungle, maybe playing mud pies and disobeying his mother, like the elephant calf Tumbi had watched the day before! Maybe—and this was a startling thought that made Tumbi's eyes widen—maybe Rajendra was a brother of the Great King! It was well possible.

Now Rajendra wore a mattress-like pad on his back to stop his harness chafing him, for he would have to bear the brunt of the coming struggle when the young captive was brought out of the trap.

Tumbi had ridden in the jeep together with Ganesha Rao and Thimme Gowda, the forestry assistant, as far as the river. The track had become worse and worse, merely a deep gully carved out by the monsoon rains every year. Wild plantains and bamboos brushed against the sides of the vehicle. The wheels skidded in the soft thick dust. Sometimes Tumbi's heart was in his mouth as the jeep lurched madly. Tumbi would infinitely have preferred to be perched on Rajendra's mountainous back than in that spluttering, roaring machine that stank of oil and gasoline!

When at last even the jeep could go no farther, Tumbi hopped out with relief. It was good to feel the earth under his bare feet again and look calmly at the sky and the trees instead of watching them whirl giddily to and fro with every hectic prancing of the jeep!

More than one prayer to the gods had silently passed Tumbi's lips on that journey.

With the two forestry officers, Tumbi waited by the river for the elephants to arrive. Silently Rajendra and his two companions padded along the soft track. It was only the men with them who made any noise. The mahouts cried to each other and the dismounted riders and attendants who accompanied them chattered loudly, speculating on the catch that awaited them. The elephants forded the river, but all those on foot had to cross by means of a narrow rope and bamboo bridge that swayed to and fro as the men pattered across. Tumbi gazed down at the muddy waters as he picked his way. He remembered the basket he had once been shown in Ganesha Rao's bungalow when he had taken another message there. It was full of rings and bangles taken from the belly of the last crocodile shot in that river.

When they had all arrived at the neighborhood of the trap, Ganesha Rao and his assistant talked with Bapundi who stood awkwardly on one foot, shy in the presence of the two men who wore clothes and shoes and thick hats. Kalyan made Rajendra kneel, and he too got down to speak with them while they discussed the coming operation.

Tumbi stood nearby, gazing down at the young elephant in the trap. He felt deeply sorry for it. That young bull must be feeling very bad, separated from his herd, his freedom a thing of the past, nothing but a life of work and captivity in front of him. Not that he could realize all that. Even so, Tumbi could not help feeling in a way awed that this young jungle creature, which one day might be magnificent, all-powerful and terrible like Rajendra or the Great King, should be taken into bondage. The elephants were so great, so strong, that there must be, there surely was, something godlike about them. Only men dared treat them in this way.

And now there was work to be done.

"Now, Tumbi," said Ganesha Rao, "take a branch and tease the young bull. But stand back from the edge of the trap, or he will get thee with his trunk."

"Lend me thy cutty!" Tumbi demanded of Gopal and, seizing the hooked knife, he quickly slashed down a long bamboo branch. With this he started to tease the young bull, who squealed angrily at him and lashed out with his trunk, the pink end of which groped up like a blind, furious hand. The teasing was to distract the elephant while other more vital things were done, for Bapundi was getting ready a specially soft rope noose which he would maneuver over the captive's head.

Meanwhile, the other men had taken their cutties and were hacking down great piles of branches and foliage which were thrown methodically into the pit. The young elephant trampled them flat as he stormed about the confines of the trap. More and more branches were thrown in, and gradually the floor of the trap was packed solid with them. Gradually, too, the level of the floor was being raised. Imperceptibly the work had its effect, and already the top of the young elephant's back was level with the brink of the pit. Slowly the captive was being brought to the surface. To and fro the sweating men toiled, chattering and squabbling about who was doing most work.

"Not even the jungle crows make so much din," shouted Ganesha Rao, hands on hips. "Swing your cutties and stay your tongues!"

Ever watchful for a furious lunge, Tumbi continued to distract the elephant by teasing him with the bamboo branch. The young bull trumpeted shrilly, snaked out his trunk, glared with his tiny eyes; and more than once Tumbi had to dart back hurriedly out of reach. While he did this, Bapundi and Gokul tried to get the noose over the elephant's head. This was a dangerous task, for they had to get as close as possible to the side of the pit, and Tumbi almost forgot his own safety as he watched Bapundi calmly and daringly playing with the rope. The little tracker and Gokul ran the rope under the elephant's neck; Gokul threw his end over to Bapundi who quickly drew the noose through the iron ring.

It was done. The noose was round the captive's neck, and the young elephant threw himself into a frenzy of rage as he felt it. That rope would have been useless if it had not been well anchored. Gopal and Govindra had seized the other end of it, and it was quickly harnessed to Rajendra, whom Kalyan had quietly ridden up close to the trap.

"Hurry, more branches!" shouted Ganesha Rao. "We must get the leg rope on!"

The men piled more branches into the pit. The elephant obligingly trampled them down solid, and slowly, inch by inch, he was brought up and up. Now Bapundi was playing with another noose, dangling it into the trap and waiting patiently for the elephant to tread in it. This was even more hazardous than getting the first noose in place, for if the elephant backed suddenly the man might be knocked into the pit and trampled to death. But Bapundi played the thick noose as unperturbed as if he were expecting to catch a mahseer in it instead of a wild elephant.

Busily Tumbi thrashed the bamboo branch about the young elephant's head, and those great feet tramped angrily here and there, crushing the branches with a furious din. Several times a hind foot trod on the noose only to shift again before Bapundi could pull it up. Bapundi grunted and spat betel juice.

Suddenly, when even Bapundi was growing weary, it happened. The elephant trod in the noose.

"*Arma!* Yes! He is caught!" The forestry assistant cried, triumphantly, and pushed back his hat.

Bapundi calmly and quickly pulled the noose tight, the young elephant struggled violently, but in vain. Now he was tethered fore and aft, and the second rope was harnessed to Tilly, who stood placidly chewing a branch of bamboo and mildly twitching her ears. Sweat gleamed on the dark skins of the men, for they had had to cut great quantities of brushwood to fill the pit. The jungle was drowsy in the afternoon heat when at last the job was done. The young elephant was out of the trap, but he was not free. Head lowered sulkily, he stood wondering what to do next. He was weary and bewildered.

He felt the rope round his neck and the rope round his hind leg, and he knew he would have to struggle against them. While the men stood around commenting on him he waited there, gathering his strength.

Tumbi watched him anxiously, hoping he would not struggle too violently, for sometimes a captive elephant got damaged if it did. Meanwhile, Ganesha Rao was checking the harness and making sure the captive showed no sign of injury. At length, on a command from the forestry officer, Kalyan gave Rajendra the order to move, and the old elephant began to amble away slowly—slowly but firmly, taking the strain of the captive's weight.

The young elephant would not budge. He stood with legs braced, refusing to be moved. Rajendra weighed more than three tons; the young bull less than half that. But Rajendra did not attempt to pull him off his feet as he could have done. He was too well trained. Now once again Tumbi marveled at the contrast between the raging Great King of yesterday and this placid, gentle old Rajendra who was so calm and patient.

The young bull had not reckoned with Tilly. Just as calmly as Rajendra, she marched up behind the captive and barged him on while Govindra directed her. Not roughly but just persuasively, she pushed him on his way. With three tons of elephant behind him, he had little choice but to move.

But if he was forced to move at all, he decided he would move fast. Suddenly, trunk up, squealing viciously, he rushed at Rajendra. His tusks were only half grown; nevertheless they could have inflicted a nasty wound. But before he could get anywhere near Rajendra, he was brought up short by that three-ton anchor behind him: at a word from Govindra, Tilly

had halted—and one ton cannot pull three tons.

Furious at this unexpected frustration, the young bull turned and tried to round on Tilly. But again, before he could get near her, he was brought to a

halt once more by the weight and strength of old Rajendra, who leaned, almost absently, on the head rope. So this tug-of-war went on for a long time amid the shouts of the men. What the young bull lacked in weight he made up for in his righteous fury at the indignity that he was suffering. For seventeen years he had roamed the jungles, feeding on the fruit of the forest, raiding the plantain gardens, feasting on pineapples, enjoying the bamboo fronds. From a hairy, helpless, comical calf that could scarcely reach his mother's nipples, he had flourished into a sizeable young bull with promising tusks. He could not think consciously of the freedom he had enjoyed, but now that he was being robbed of it he fought for it with every muscle and nerve and fiber of his being.

He had given up his angry squealing; that was a waste of breath. Even the two powerful camp elephants had to work hard to subdue their raging captive. To and fro they tramped and trudged in this battle of wills and giant bodies, while the mahouts sat up there on high, touching their mounts with a heel or giving them a sharp order.

Breathlessly Tumbi watched. His feelings were torn. He felt deeply sorry for the young bull now being dragged from his freedom in all the mystery of the jungle. On the other hand, he felt deep admiration for the fact that men could bring out all the sagacity and working powers of the elephant, as they would with this, the latest victim of Bapundi's cunning.

# 5

*A new life begins*

It was a long march through the jungle. Hauled on
by Rajendra, pushed by Tilly, urged on noisily and
beaten with sticks by the men, the young bull dis-
puted every step of the way until he lapsed into a
sullen stupor, not understanding what was happening
to him. Sometimes the men had to scatter quickly as
he lunged sideways at them before the camp elephants
could check him. Once he caught Gopal a swipe with
his trunk which bowled the fellow over into a thorn
bush, where he sat shrieking as if a leopard were claw-

ing him, which made even Ganesha Rao laugh, for
Gopal was notorious for always getting into trouble.
He was more hurt by the thorns than by the young
elephant's trunk, for luckily it was a glancing blow,
else he would have had no sense left even to feel the
thorns.

It was a long march through the jungle, but why
tell of all the captive's humiliation as he was bustled
into bondage? The jungle watched him go for the
last time. The flower peckers uttered their sharp
*chik-chik-chik* as if in disapproval of what was happening. The flame-of-the-forest petals fluttered to
the ground, perhaps at the flap of a waxbill's wing,
perhaps in sorrow. Never again would the young
bull pass that way, except maybe in years to come to
help drag another captive from the jungle.

When at length, the weary day nearly done, the
camp was reached, he had to be put into one of the
teakwood cages, where he would fret for some three
weeks while the fiery spirit gradually evaporated
from him like sap from a damaged tree, and he became resigned to being enslaved by man. Now
Krishna was brought up to help. While Rajendra
continued to act as anchor, Tilly and Krishna closed
in on each side of the young bull, and he was marched
towards the stockade. The solid tree trunks that
formed the front of the cage had been slipped out of

63

their sockets. At the entrance, Tilly was unharnessed from the captive, and Krishna alone, ridden by Tipane, marched him into the cage which was just wide enough to accommodate them both.

"Now we must work fast!" ordered Ganesha Rao, climbing up the side of the cage to see how things were doing. "Lash the bull to the side bars and undo Krishna."

Quickly the mahouts did as they were told. Daringly Gokul worked in the cage, a pigmy against the huge bulk of Krishna. Now the rope that had been harnessed to Rajendra was taken round one of the thick bars. Krishna was unleased from the side of the captive, and at a signal from Tipane, he began to shuffle out backwards.

"Put the bars in place!" ordered Ganesha Rao, as soon as Krishna had emerged. The teakwood bars were enormously heavy, and the men grunted as they lifted them into place. Tumbi helped, and the sweat ran over him as if his skin had been polished. When the lower bars had been replaced, the higher ones, which had to be removed because of Krishna's height, had to be hauled up by ropes. Bapundi scaled the cage as nimbly as a monkey to adjust them.

When all had been done, Gokul released the noose from the young bull. If he had been worn out by the long march through the jungle, he took on a fresh burst of energy now. He squealed defiantly, bashed his forehead against the bars, kicked out with his forefeet. But all this made no impression on the teakwood: it, too, had been fashioned over many years by the same hand that had wrought the young bull and endowed him with his strength. At Kalyan's order, Tumbi had gone off to cut bamboo branches for the newcomer. He stuffed these through the bars, but the young bull merely snatched them viciously and trampled them unappreciatively to shreds.

Tumbi watched him sympathetically.

"When thou art big enough to work," he said, "I shall be chief mahout of this camp and will ride upon thy back. I will carry a jeweled ankus, and thou shalt wear a golden bell with a note softer than the croodling of a dove!"

Tumbi's eloquence was wasted. The elephant poked his trunk through the bars and blew a great blast of wet dust at the boy, spattering him from head to foot.

All the mahouts laughed mightily at that, and the young bull's trumpeting mingled with their laughter.

Tumbi raised a hand in angry gesture as he sprang back, eyes flashing.

"Hai! Thou art a *makhna!*" he shouted. "Thou wilt never grow tusks!"

"Look closely, Tumbi," said Ganesha Rao, dryly, "and thou wilt see he is no *makhna*."

"Indeed, that is so," Tumbi agreed ruefully. "Those tusks could already kill a man."

Meanwhile, the previous victim of Bapundi's skill, a very young cow elephant, had been released from her cage and was chained between two tree stumps. She had been caught a fortnight before and could now be fed by hand. Now the time had come to start giving her instruction, and the best way of doing that was to take her to the river for a bath, where she would have to learn to obey the commands of men.

The following day, the great camp elephants once again ambled up to act as escorts. It was they, too, who had dragged the young cow from the jungle when she was caught. Quietly and expertly, with an air almost of regret, as if they realized what it all meant (and who shall say they did not know?), they wheeled into place at a touch of their riders' feet. One on either side of the little cow they moved, closer and closer but with infinite care, so that she almost disappeared between their towering frames.

She squealed peevishly and tried to struggle against her chain, but her two instructors gently went on crowding her in until she had to submit.

Tumbi had run to fetch a lump of sweet jaggery

and now, while the two massive trunks dangled on either side of him, he fed pieces to the young cow to distract her while a rope noose, with a large wooden peg in it to stop its shocking her, was harnessed on her.

"Eat! Take and eat!" Tumbi urged her, though she needed no urging. "Here is sweetness to soften thine anger."

Next a leather-padded chain was attached to her hind leg and the other end to Rajendra. Then the chain was unshackled from the tree stumps, and she was ready for her first walk to the river, her first walk since she had been captured.

Now it was an easier walk than the last march through the jungle. The three big elephants were keen to get down to the river, and their young pupil was too small to argue. Eagerly Tumbi and Gokul and the rest followed, for it was always an event when a captive elephant was exercised for the first time. Unheedful of the blanket of dust that rose behind the posse of elephants, the men pattered on. The bells clanged and jingled—Rajendra's clonked dully —and that was the only sound. Like figures in a dream, the elephants floated away through the haze of dust.

"Truly they are splendid, these giants who move as silently as a cloud," thought Tumbi. It was indeed almost frightening the way these gigantic animals could at times move like shadows. Were it not for their bells, they could steal up behind a man as unperceived as his conscience.

When they came to the river, all four elephants waded out.

"Undo Krishna and Tilly," ordered Kalyan from Rajendra's back. The camp attendants did as they were ordered, and now the young cow was tethered only by the head rope to Rajendra, who stood knee-deep with his trunk draped over a tusk, like some old gentleman carrying his coat on his arm. Rajendra looked utterly bored.

Slightly bewildered, the young cow stood in the middle of the river with plenty of slack on the rope that held her. Tumbi tucked up his *dhoti* securely and, with Gokul and half a dozen others, waded out after her. She turned on them at first, but Rajendra, without waiting for a word from Kalyan, simply reminded her that it would be an uncomfortable business if she started to argue with him.

With blows of their hands and sticks they had picked up on the way, the men began to beat the young cow. The blows rattled and smacked on her gray hide, but it would have taken more than that to hurt her, even at her age.

"*But-but-but-but-but!*" the men began to chant

in a rapid chorus. This was elephant language, Hindi, in fact, which all mahouts used in their work, whatever their own language. *"But-but-but-but-but! Sit!"* The quick-fire chorus went on, to the accompaniment of the smacks and blows.

For a long time, the young cow struggled and resisted. Rajendra even had to drop his bored pose for a while to deal with her firmly as she tramped and heaved in the flowing water.

*"But-but-but-but!"* Tumbi and the others urged unremittingly, whacking away with hand and stick.

They laughed merrily as they belabored their stubborn pupil. They must not give in now, or she would never obey. Perhaps the jungle spirit in her was putting up its final resistance. She could not help being captured, but once in captivity, she could resist. An elephant that would not obey would be useless as a worker.

But it was no use. The will of man was stronger than the jungle spirit. Suddenly in the trees, there was a raucous shriek. It was in fact the cry of a rose-ringed parakeet, but it might well have been the jungle spirit giving up in despair. At any rate, the young cow at last obeyed the men. Ponderously, with an air of resignation, she sank down in the water.

At once a shout of mingled triumph and approbation went up from the men.

"*Sabbash, bettah!*" Tumbi cried, grinning from ear to ear.

"*Sabbash, bettah!*" the mahouts echoed. "Well done, brother!" It mattered not if in fact she was a sister, the men were genuinely enthusiastic that she had done what they had been exhorting her to do. That was the first order she had ever obeyed and therefore the most important one. It was only a simple lesson, yet from now on life for the young cow would never be the same.

Fondly Tumbi and the men began to splash water over her wrinkled gray side, and she began to enjoy the experience. But then she floundered up again, tried a last time to break loose, only to be reminded of her impotence by Rajendra, on whose back gray-headed Kalyan now sat sideways to watch the lesson.

"*But-but-but-but!*" the elephant language chorus started again. So did the beating of sticks and the smacking of hands. For a while, the young cow straddled morosely there while the idea of what the men wanted sank in.

Then another ponderous splash and she sank down again and once more a delighted cry of "*Sabbash, bettah!*"

"Is she not an apt pupil, *doringlee?*" Tumbi cried to Ganesha Rao, standing on the bank.

71

"Truly, she will make a good worker," agreed the forestry officer, tilting his pith helmet against the sun.

Briskly the men began to scrub the young cow as she sprawled there hugely in the river. She made no attempt to get up this time and lay there contentedly. But now she learnt bitterly the contrariness of her new masters. No sooner had she settled herself comfortably with the cool water flowing round her than the men were at her again, beating her with sticks and smacking her with disrespectful hands.

"*Oot-oot-oot-oot!*" they commanded her now. "Get up! Get up!"

Indeed, there was no peace for those who became the thralls of men.

# 6

*The Great King goes raiding*

It was not long after this that the Great King started to become troublesome. For the time being, he had left the herd, as old bulls often would, and went in solitary company with a young bull, one of his sons. Food was hard to find, for every year men were felling the jungle, clearing it for their terraced paddy fields and their ragi (seed) and gram. The kingdom of the elephants was shrinking under axe and fire. The rasp of the saw was heard more often than the rasping cough of the panther; the yelp of the pariah dog more often than the bark of the muntjac deer.

For a while, Tumbi had gone to live in the village a few miles from the elephant camp. He did so at his widowed mother's request, for her brother, who kept her, needed help to thresh the first cut of paddy. This had to be done in a hurry, as Tumbi's uncle had borrowed a team of bullocks from his neighbor to tread out the pale brown straw, trudging endlessly round while Tumbi urged them on.

But Tumbi and his mother also worked on a neighboring coffee estate, where, during the harvest, he could earn as much as two rupees a day picking the shining red and green berries.

Every evening, the pickers trooped back to the drying ground with their gunnysacks of berries, eager to get them weighed and see what they had earned. Men and women and children squatted on the barbecue, sorting out the ripe from the unripe and chattering like mynahs about how much they had picked and what they intended to do with their money when the harvest was done. All round the barbecue the bougainvillea blossomed, a garland of color enclosing all the many colors of the women's saris, green and red and purple and ochre. The women worked faster than the men, for their hands were defter. The bangles on their wrists flashed and jingled as they worked.

74

"This is not a man's work," grumbled Tumbi, as he squatted there in the lengthening shadows cast by the jacaranda trees. "I would sooner wash Rajendra thrice in one day than sit fiddling with these berries. Surely a man earns every anna he makes at this work!"

"Thou wouldst soon starve, son," his mother said, tartly, "if the pace of thy work was always so slow. A water buffalo would sort these berries quicker than thou dost!"

While Tumbi was thinking of a suitable retort, there was a sudden shout from somewhere in the coffee estate. At first nobody took any notice among the chattering of the pickers, but Tumbi paused and pricked up his ears.

The cry was repeated, and Tumbi sprang to his feet.

"Elephant!" he said, staring urgently in the direction of the cry. "Someone shouts that there is an elephant!"

A moment later, a man burst out of the bushes on the far side of the drying ground, where the previous day's picking was spread out.

"*Rumba peria ani!*" he yelled, his eyes rolling with fear, sweat on his face. "A very big tusker!"

Gradually the chattering ceased but was taken up again immediately as the news spread. The workers stood up in a sudden rustling wave of color and stared fearfully.

"He is huge, I tell you!" the newsbearer cried, holding the skirt of his *dhoti*. He was one of the estate clerks. "I have never seen so big an elephant, and his tusks were longer than the shaft of a bullock cart!"

For a long time nothing happened, and some people began to say that the man was telling lies, that there was no elephant. Tumbi had left the barbecue and gone towards the plantation. He knew the man was not lying, for he could hear a great body moving about under the shade trees that sheltered the coffee bushes. Then he caught sight of a massive gray form tramping steadily on, barging its way through the close-set ranks of coffee.

Tumbi would have known that figure anywhere.

"It is the Great King!" he shouted, though nobody knew what he meant. The Great King was just any elephant to the villagers. It was only the elephant men of Kadanga who gave him his title. Out of the estate the old elephant marched, stained all manner of hues from red to gray by the accumulated dust of many decades.

He was not interested in the coffee, but he knew that beyond the estate there were some excellent plantains, even the pineapples were ripening, and there were oranges, too. The Great King's belly was empty, and it needed a lot of filling.

In vain did the overseers try to calm the workers. Shrieking wildly, gathering their saris about them, the women fled; and many of the men were not long in following suit. They huddled down in the shelter of the labor lines and kept fearful watch. There would be some fine disputes later on when it came to sorting out the day's picking.

A quarter of a mile away, the Great King marched on through a little valley, followed now by the young bull. Meanwhile, the alarm had been raised in the village and, anxious for their crops, men rushed out with long cattle horns and drums and even old kerosene tins. The din was like the frenzied music of some senseless rite.

Tumbi rushed down toward the village. He met his uncle struggling up the hill with the team of bullocks. The old man was terrified that the elephants might injure them and his neighbor hold him responsible, for he was already deeply in debt.

"Fear not, uncle mine," Tumbi grinned. "The Great King will eat thy plantains but not Chowdappa's bullocks."

They drove the bullocks up the hill and tethered them to some palm trees, and they hurried back to help drive the elephants away from the tiny fields near the village. There was so much noise from cattle horns and drums and screaming voices that even the Great King had second thoughts. Tumbi could see him in a patch of scrub jungle, standing among the plantana bushes with great ears alert, clearly sizing up the prospects.

The men with the cattle horns had climbed for safety into the nearest trees and sat astride the branches blowing stridently or urging each other to be bold and pursue the elephants. At last the Great King and his companion drifted away, and the noises gradually subsided. One by one the men climbed down from the perches and listened uneasily.

"They have taken themselves off," Tumbi re-assured them presently, returning from a cautious reconnaissance. Each man boasting of the part he had played in driving the monstrous elephants off, the villagers dispersed. Timidly the women emerged from their mud-walled houses to fetch water from the well. Up on the barbecue angry groups of men and women were shrilly accusing each other of filching their coffee. The agitated overseer sent a peon off to the bungalow to fetch the white planter to deal with the situation.

The Great King had not given up his intention of raiding the plantains. As soon as the tropical night had come down and the cowdung fires were burning and the jackals were shrieking, he and the young bull came back quietly and stripped the plantain groves and pilfered many oranges. Nobody knew they had returned until it was too late.

Well satisfied, the Great King, attended by his son, marched up the hill and passed the coffee go-downs on the way. Evidently he was now in good humor, having a moderately full belly, for he began to rip the roof from one of the godowns. By now Ram, one of the watchmen, had raised the alarm, and once more men swarmed out to try to drive the elephants off with their cacophony of drums and horns, but in the darkness, they dared not approach too closely.

By the flickering light of a dozen brands, the men stood watching the Great King's antics. The elephant had torn off a sheet of corrugated iron, which went slithering and crashing away. Then he began to explore inside the little building with his trunk. That trunk seemed to be an entity all on its own, a blind, groping yet uncannily expert hand. It went probing and exploring, snuffing the sacks of coffee. It came across a crate which it proceeded to pick up and drop. The crate crashed to the floor. The Great King picked it up again, let it drop once more. The game seemed to amuse him. He went on picking up the flimsy crate and dropping it until it split open.

The crate was full of watering cans, half a dozen of them. The Great King picked up a can and flipped it over his shoulder. It landed with a clanking rattle, and the old elephant turned and, striding after it, crushed it flat with his foot as if displeased with the noise it made. Now his son took a turn at the game. He too put his trunk through the roof, picked up a watering can, pitched it a few yards and then trampled on it.

All this time, the din of horns and drums and tins went on, the lighted brands flickered and spat, and the snaking light gleamed on the bodies of the men as they stood in wonder watching the elephants amusing themselves so insolently. Time after time, the Great King snatched a watering can and chucked it mischievously away, only to trample it flat with one neat blow of his foot.

"Truly the elephants have invented a new game," whispered Tumbi to his uncle.

The old man drew in a quavering breath. It seemed to him almost as if the gods were besporting themselves.

At last, however, the game palled—or perhaps the supply of watering cans came to an end. The two elephants wandered off, but at that distance and in the uncertain light of the torches, nobody was certain which way they had gone, nor did any man fancy trying to find out. Anxiously the villagers returned to their homes, prepared to defend their crops through the night. The watchmen on the coffee estate built big fires to give themselves courage.

The Great King did not come back that night. But Tumbi knew he was not far away. He could sense the elephant's presence.

Next day nobody could talk of anything but the elephants. Men and women watched the jungle fearfully. When the women went out with their baskets to gather cattle dung for fuel, they made a boy keep watch for them.

"We must make *pooja* to the gods," said the village headman, "and place offerings on the shrines so that they will be propitiated and command the elephants not to harm us."

As it happened, a *sadhu*, a holy man, wearing a dirty saffron-colored robe and with sacred ash marks on his forehead and a mad look in his eyes, had come to the village that morning. Leaning on his staff, he trudged barefoot from door to door holding out his begging bowl.

It was not difficult, on certain conditions, of course, to prevail upon the holy man to make a really powerful *pooja* to the gods. This he did, while the village gathered round in awe at such a *sadhu* who could say such marvelous things, even if not one man among them could understand what he said. On the *sadhu's* instructions, the villagers placed offerings of fruit and grain at the village shrine, a little stoop-high oblong of stones guarded by terra-cotta horses. Tumbi's uncle had no fruit left, but he brought sweet-scented frangipani flowers instead.

"Dost thou think thou art a priest that thou canst bring flowers of the temple tree?" sneered his neighbor, Chowdappa.

"Why should some bring only flowers while we sacrifice our finest fruit to the gods?" scolded Aurobindo Woodcutter's wife, who had brought oranges her children had stolen.

That night the Great King visited the shrine. But not to make *pooja* to the gods. The fruit was good, but it was not enough.

In the evening, confident that with the aid of the holy man (who had never eaten so much curry in all his life) they would be secure, the villagers returned from work. The scrawny, humpbacked, sacred little cows were herded back from their everlasting search for grazing, the women walked gracefully from the wells with the brass chatties balanced nonchalantly on their well-oiled, flower-decked heads, the men squatted outside their mud huts gossiping of this and that, mainly of money and crops and their wives.

When night fell and the geckos were hiccuping

and the crickets crying like tiny bells, they went in-
doors and gathered round the cow dung fires. The
wife of Aurobindo Woodcutter was lucky. She had
a fire of wood, over which she cooked the evening
meal. Her hut was the last in the village, and every
day Aurobindo took his bullock cart out into the
forest and gathered fuel which he sold at an exorbi-
tant price.

Now while he squatted playing with his son, the
woman boiled the supper rice and prepared the vege-
tables to go with it. Suddenly she heard a soft footstep
outside. She took little notice of it at first, vaguely
thinking it was her neighbor passing by or a stray
cow. Next moment she shrieked piercingly and
dropped the pot. A huge trunk had come snaking
through the unglazed window, seeking what it could
find.

The Great King had come marching by, on the
way to raid the fruit groves, when a good smell at-
tracted him to the woodcutter's hut. Aurobindo
sprang to his feet, transfixed and terrified. As for the
woman, she came to her senses first, snatched up a
brand from the fire and thrust it at the groping trunk.

The Great King uttered a squeal of pain and
anger and went storming off towards the jungle.
Fearfully the woodcutter's family rushed out of the
hut to make certain where he had gone. They could

hear him crashing away wildly in the distance. Other villagers had hurried out at the noise of the commotion.

"Suddenly there was the trunk," the woman babbled, as they discussed the matter over and over again. "It would have stolen all I had put by for the morrow's food, but I seized a brand from the fire and burned him with it."

"Thou must build an elephant trench about thy house, Aurobindo!" someone advised.

"No need for a trench now," said another. "That elephant will think twice ere he returns. Truly he has been taught a lesson, better than any *pooja!*"

Standing at the edge of the chattering group, Tumbi frowned. He thought it wrong that the Great King had been insulted.

# 7

*Vengeance*

The coffee harvest was over. Tumbi had made good money, but he would be glad to return to the elephant camp. The evening that the casual workers lined up on the drying ground to receive their final pay and leave their thumbprints in receipt, a wandering snake charmer happened to pass through the village.

"Beware!" said Lal, the storekeeper. "He hopes to charm the money from you with his music."

"If thou hast left us any when we have bought

thy wares at extortionate prices," retorted Shriedram Washerman.

"Begone, thou insolent pollution!" yelled Lal, waving the *dhobi* off. "It is cloth for *dhotis* and *cholis* that I sell most, because thou ruinest the clothes with thy banging and rubbing against the stones. Buy some of my fine sandalwood soap and thy customers would be better pleased."

Meanwhile, the snake charmer, a tall, bearded man with a pink turban and an ingratiating manner, stood around on one leg, scratching it with the big toe of his other foot and waiting hopefully for the villagers to take an interest. With uneasy eyes the passersby glanced at the little round lidded basket and the sack that lay at his feet. They knew the man's profession, for he held his calabash pipe, decorated with silver, in one hand and sometimes played an inviting, reedy note upon it.

"Hast thou pulled out the cobra's fangs?" Tumbi asked, smiling with the satisfaction of one who had tied a nice bundle of rupee notes in a corner of his dhoti. "Or dost thou make him chew blanket all day long to rid him of his poison?"

"Wilt thou try?" challenged the snake charmer, stooping as if to raise the lid of the basket, at which Tumbi discreetly stepped back a pace. "I have been bitten many times, but I use the root *nirvasi* to protect me against ill effects. Ground to a powder and mixed with ghee, it is an infallible cure. Very rare is this root, but as a mark of friendship to this village I am willing to part with a little . . . at a certain price."

The snake charmer spoke in a lofty tone as a professional addressing the ignorant.

By now several more villagers had begun to gather round curiously, and the snake charmer warmed to the task of rousing his audience's interest.

"I am of the Jogi Jat," he announced, proudly, "protectors of the snakes. I am fully qualified as snake charmer. See! Here is my diploma!"

Taking a little bamboo tube from inside his shirt, he tapped one end and out fell a rolled-up piece of paper which he proceeded to unfold, though as scarcely anyone in the village could read, it might have been a government decree or an election address for all the villagers knew.

However, the Jogi Jat by now had the promise of an audience willing to pay for their entertainment, and he squatted down on the stone platform under the holy peepul tree, the village meeting place, ready to start his performance.

It was noticeable that no one else squatted near him. A few daring souls such as Tumbi perched on the edge of the platform, but most of the audience preferred to stand out of range of any possible mishap. Though they had nodded knowingly at Tumbi's quips, a snake was a snake and not to be taken on trust, creature of the gods though it was.

The snake charmer began by muttering an incantation. It was impossible to understand what he was saying, and of course it was all the more impressive because of that. Then cautiously he lifted the lid of the basket a little and, leaning over it, hissed loudly to arouse the cobra. Now he took his bulging pipe in both hands and set it to his bearded lips. The music he played was not nice. It was high-pitched and weird, and it seemed that the notes crawled into the air like wriggling, invisible snakes; and Tumbi shuddered as he sat there, arms round knees.

With parted lips and uneasy eyes, the villagers watched. There were only men in the audience. The women were too busy, carrying water from the well or gathering cow dung for the fire or cooking the evening meal.

Slowly the cobra responded to the music of its master. Redolent of all the mystery of existence to which man strove eternally to find the answer, the cobra wavered slowly up from the basket, its hood expanded, its tongue flickering back and forth. It was a drab brown in color, but on the back of its hood were two rings of the most beautiful milky blue. Not the sky nor a bird's egg nor a butterfly's wing nor any flower possessed that same innocent tone of blue which adorned this deadly creature.

To and fro the snake began to sway as it came under the influence of the music, and while he played

away on his pipe, the snake charmer rhythmically worked one knee round and round as if to work the eerie tune out of his body.

For a while the cobra sat up attentively as the monotonous, unpleasant music droned on, but presently the snake charmer drew it right out of the basket and made it move backwards across the peepul-tree platform away from him.

Tumbi jumped off the edge of the stone platform. The circle of onlookers receded imperceptibly. Like a tide, they moved back again when the snake charmer made the cobra go towards him again. Backwards and forwards the swaying snake and the watchful audience moved in unconscious rhythm. It was as if the shrill music had everyone under its spell.

Now the Jogi Jat made the snake return to its basket, guiding it, hissing, with a waving hand and the ceaseless music. The sinister hood subsided, the neat coils sank down into the basket and the man replaced the lid. Eagerly Tumbi and the villagers pressed against the parapet of the platform and watched as he undid the sack. They could tell that there was a much larger snake in this.

Out of the sack writhed a ten-foot dhamin or rat snake. It was harmless, but the audience chewed their betel nut earnestly as it proceeded to climb over its master's knee and wind itself caressingly round his waist, over his arms and about his neck. Here and there it glided, while the man swayed his body in response. Now the snake tired of the game and went sinuously and rapidly across the ground while men trod on each other's toes in their anxiety to get out of the way. The snake charmer trapped the snake's tail between his toes, and the dhamin turned swiftly on him, leaping several feet in the air toward him so that the snake charmer had to spring back out of reach.

Again and again this happened, and it was an impressive trick, even though the snake had no poison fangs. It was terrifying to see the snake spring like a four-footed creature.

"Now I will exhibit both my snakes together," announced the snake charmer; "but first I must borrow needle and cotton, for I have lost mine."

"What should a snake charmer do with needle and thread?" grumbled Lal, but he went to his shop to fetch them, for he wanted value for the rupee he had promised for the performance.

When Lal returned with the needle and cotton, the stranger took the dhamin firmly just below the head and began to stitch its mouth up, while the snake vainly wrapped itself round his waist.

"His mouth must be sewn thus," explained the snake charmer, as he squatted under the peepul tree; "else he would swallow the cobra."

This done, he resumed his performance. The rat snake showed no resentment at its brutal treatment and, while the cobra once more swayed languidly upwards at the beckoning of the pipe, it wavered and writhed over the arms and shoulders of the snake charmer, whose eyes gleamed intently in the fading light.

At last the music faltered to a close, the audience relaxed and manifested its relief by a widespread spitting of betel juice. Magnanimously Tumbi led the contributions with a rupee note. The man placed his hands together before his face in a gesture of thanks.

"A little milk for my snakes, friends," he wheedled. "And some rice and chapaties for myself. I have not eaten since dawn, and I traveled far from my road especially to visit your honored village and show my humble skill."

"Hadst thou perchance heard that there was money in the village at the end of the coffee harvest?" asked someone sarcastically.

Now the fireflies were beginning to weave their bright pattern through the cool air. In the paddy fields, frogs were conversing. The cicadas kept up their endless reeling in the tamarinds where the monkeys sat gravely listening to the men and pretending they could understand. With one or two villagers, Tumbi strolled away to squat for a while with

Narayan the watchman, who had lit a log fire at the edge of the estate road. A bullock cart went creaking by, and the eyes of the bullocks shone green as emeralds in the light as they passed. From the axle a lantern hung, but unlit.

"Truly there are safer ways of earning one's livelihood than by fondling snakes," said Narayan, as they squatted there eating the oranges that he was supposed to guard.

"Such men are snake-worshippers," said Shried-ram Washerman. "Every year they hold a great feast when they honor the snakes and take offerings of milk and plantains to them in their homes in the ant hills."

"Undoubtedly the snake is a holy creature," observed someone, his face gleaming in the light of the fire. "Was it not on the coils of Subramaniah, the great serpent, that the Lord Vishnu reclined while he slept upon the sea?"

"Ram the Brahmin leaves a patch uncut in his garden so that the cobra that lives there may come and go undisturbed," said someone else.

The talk continued until the fire died down and the men drifted away to their homes. Narayan took a lighted brand and started out on his rounds through the estate. Now that the coffee had been harvested, there remained only the oranges to guard.

93

As Tumbi hurried towards his uncle's house, slightly anxious now that he had left the comforting ring of fire, he thought eagerly of the elephant camp. Tomorrow he would return there, and he would be glad to be among the elephants again and the men who worked with them. He did not like the village; here men were too quarrelsome and grasping. Nobody spoke well of his neighbor. Nobody thought of anything but money. He would give all the money he had earned at the coffee-picking to his mother. He needed none in the jungle.

All at once his meditating was interrupted. Jackals were screaming on the edge of the village. Out of the trees a stray cow came trotting, her bell ringing urgently, her hipbones sticking up like clothes pegs. She had been forgotten when the village herd was driven home. At first Tumbi thought the cow was frightened of the jackals, but the jackals themselves were yelping in a strange tone.

The boy halted and listened. Was it panther or tiger? Sometimes they came that way. Only a month ago a tiger had lifted two bullocks. His heart began to thump loudly as he stared into the darkness. But he told himself that the jackals would not call like that were it a tiger. They would be screaming in that awful voice that presaged a kill. He listened attentively, every sense alert. Now he knew. It was an elephant that was moving somewhere over there in the darkness of the trees. A big elephant marching steadily through the strip of scrub jungle near the estate. It was making little attempt at keeping quiet and strode on resolutely.

It could be only one certain elephant; none other.

"It is the Great King," Tumbi muttered to himself and drew in his breath with a sharp hiss of apprehension. There was no doubt about it. The Great King was marching on the village.

Fearfully Tumbi pattered on and kept track of the elephant. He waited to see which way the old bull would go, ready if necessary to run and warn his mother. But the Great King, a starkly looming hulk of shadow, strode past several huts and fields without taking any notice of them. In the bamboo cattle sheds, bells rang faintly and anxiously as the cows caught the scent of the elephant. A pariah dog went whimpering across the road. The jackals shrieked in the distance.

Now Tumbi guessed what the Great King was about. The elephant made his way parallel to the dirt road, toward the end of the village. He was going back to Aurobindo Woodcutter's house to seek vengeance for the hurt and indignity he had suffered when the housewife burned his trunk. Nothing would stop the elephant now he had that idea in his head.

Other villagers had heard the elephant now, and they rushed out shouting the alarm. But the Great King kept straight on, and certainly there was no man who dared cross his path. Lying asleep on the floor, Aurobindo and his family snored contentedly, their bellies full of rice, thanks to the price of fire-wood. They awoke with gasps and shrieks to find the roof of their hut being ripped off. They sprang up and ran outside, the woman screaming shrilly, the children yelling.

The Great King took a swift revenge. Against his mighty bulk, the woodcutter's hut was of no avail. He tore down the bamboo thatch, battered his great head against the mud walls, pushed his way into what had once been a home, trampled on pots and scant possessions.

When he had done what he had set out to do, he went away again without touching anyone else's property. Aurobindo Woodcutter and his family had to seek shelter with their relations that night. Many times in the future Aurobindo attempted to repair his house, but each time, sooner or later, the Great King came back to it and did more damage, until at last the woodcutter was forced to build a new hut somewhere else. This time he took the precaution of

digging an elephant trench around his dwelling.

It was a long time before men ceased to marvel at the way the Great King had returned to seek his revenge. Tumbi did not marvel: he knew the mind of the elephants, and he marveled only that they would bend their knee at a word from a man.

# 8

*Strong as gods*

There was much to be done in the camp, and each day was a long day. When the jungle mists were still netted in the branches of the stinkwood trees and the little jungle cocks were hiccuping nervously, the mahouts had to set out in search of their elephants. It was a time when the night hunters encountered the day workers, the most breathless moment in the jungle, when you were as likely to stumble upon a sounder of wild pigs as catch a glimpse of a panther skulking back to his lair after hiding his catch in the fork of a tree to protect it from scavengers.

The coppersmith bird started his monotonous tonking. The gray hornbill chattered raucously as he went in search of mud with which to wall up his nesting mate. The spotted doves croodled affectionately as the brittle sunlight—fresh and fragrant and magical as it never would be later on in the stunning heat of full day—broke like a cascade of music through the network of branches.

Sometimes Tumbi went out with Kalyan in search of Rajendra. To begin with, it was easy to follow the track of the elephant. Kalyan knew his spoor at a glance, even among that of many other elephants; moreover, you could see where Rajendra had pulled down a mouthful or two of bamboo or kicked over an anthill. Presently, however, it became more difficult. Despite the impediment of the chain attached to one foot, the elephant could still get about without undue difficulty, and he knew that the farther he went the longer it would take to find him, and the longer it took to find him the shorter would be the working day.

It was Rajendra's cracked bell that Kalyan and Tumbi listened for, just as the other mahouts traced their elephants by the individual bells. But even where the bell was concerned, Rajendra was cunning beyond belief. Sometimes the bell would be oddly silent; it was as if the elephant had vanished in the depths of the jungle. At such a time it might be two hours or more before Kalyan traced his mount, for the wily Rajendra had filled the bell with mud so that it would not ring.

"Truly thou art akin to the crocodile in thy cunning," Kalyan would chide him then, and the elephant would gently but mischievously impede the man with his trunk as the mahout cleaned out the bell.

Whenever Kalyan did begin to locate Rajendra, he would call to him from a distance and coax him into the right mood. "Come along! Come along!" he would cry as casually as if he were simply calling a humpbacked cow to be milked. "Is there no limit to the depth of thy belly, old father?" Kalyan would shout. "There is work to be done, thou idle-back!"

Rajendra took his time, especially if he had wandered along the riverbank to feed among the succulent grass. He was very fastidious about his food. He wrapped his trunk dexterously round a tuft of grass, pulled it up and beat soil and roots against his foot before stuffing the tuft into his mouth. Maybe something displeased him about it, in which case he would put his foot on the tuft he had gathered and draw his curled trunk away from it.

Invariably he had to have a good scratch before

he started work. He leaned his enormous rump on an unfortunate tree and grunted with pleasure as he rubbed ponderously against it. Sometimes a tree was not quite right, and he would pick up a sizeable stick in his trunk and scratch his flank with that. Then he expelled the breath from his mighty lungs in a great hissing gasp, as if with a sigh of satisfaction.

At last, knowing full well that his mahout's patience had a limit, he would condescend to shuffle reluctantly to work.

When Kalyan had taken the chain from his leg, Rajendra would put out one forefoot sideways in obedience to a command. The old mahout stepped on it, as if on a mounting block, and Rajendra lifted his leg up as high as he could while Kalyan scrambled quickly on to his back. Tumbi grinned in approval of this trick. Usually the elephants sat down, with legs stretched out fore and aft, while their riders mounted, but this was a special trick Kalyan had taught Rajendra many years ago.

Once he got to work, Rajendra, like the other camp elephants, worked willingly enough, though of course he must first have his morning ration of rice and jaggery. One day, when Kalyan was in a bad temper after having searched a long time for Rajendra, he started to march the elephant off to work without his proper breakfast. Rajendra refused to go, and when Kalyan tried to force him, he became very angry and hurled lumps of dung at the mahout. Worst of all, he hit Ganesha Rao who was standing near.

Now, laden with great dragging chains and with a thick pad on his shoulders to protect him from the pull of the chains, Rajendra strode off at the head of the work gang towards the teak plantation where they were operating.

Tumbi worked with the sawyers. Once the trees were felled, every branch and jag had to be cut from the trunk; otherwise they might catch in the under-growth and impede the hauling. Holes had to be bored through the thinner end of each tree trunk, too, so that the dragging gear could be attached.

Now Tumbi and one of the sawyers gathered the ends of Rajendra's chains and coupled them with an iron pin through the dragging hole in one of the trees. Solid and heavy was the teakwood; it was like the elephants themselves, and Tumbi felt a strange satisfaction as he ran a hand along it. All trees were wonderful, and living creatures though they could not move from place to place. They gave shelter to the birds who sang in thanks for this. They provided fruit for the monkeys. They provided a place for the bees to make their honeycombs or for the hornets to hang their huge nests. They provided timber for men's houses and bridges that spanned the rivers. The twigs and branches provided fuel. The great roots sucked up the monsoon rains and protected the soil which would otherwise have been washed away as it was in places where the trees had vanished.

Ganesha Rao, the forestry officer, had often spoken of all this to Tumbi, when he saw that the boy was interested. There was much more, too, about trees.

It was while sitting under a tree that Gautama Buddha had received enlightenment. The bards who composed the Vedas sang of the beautiful trees and stately forests. The great Upanishads were written among the cool forest retreats. In paradise, the fabulous kalpa tree put forth golden fruit with an exquisite flavor.

But Tumbi was not concerned with all this. He did know that the trees were splendid and majestic, so big they must belong to the gods, just as the elephants did. All things that were big or powerful were worthy of being worshipped as gods. Even the venomous snake that lurked in the forest glades was worthy to be so regarded, for had it not the power to kill most swiftly?

"Haul! Haul proudly, old father!" shouted Tumbi to Rajendra. "Birds have sung in the branches of this tree."

At a word from Kalyan, Rajendra began to pull. He leaned on his harness to test the weight of the tree, for he must judge what power to exert. For a moment the felled tree resisted, as if reluctant to leave the forest where it had grown from a tiny seed, but then with a grunt Rajendra hauled manfully and the tree rustled and thudded through the undergrowth.

"Pull, then! Pull!" urged Kalyan from on high, while Tumbi echoed his words alongside the straining elephant. Rajendra halted to get his second wind and then once again set off.

"Pull, thou idle-back!" shouted the mahout and Rajendra answered, perhaps indignant at such imputations, with a loud squeal as he got into his stride. His cracked bell jingled, the chains clanked and the tree glided along slowly but smoothly.

Through the jungle the elephant strained, his mighty body pitted against the mighty tree. Every now and then he paused to rest, for even Rajendra's muscles ached at times. It was strange, though, how this always seemed to happen within reach of a cluster of bamboo or a stretch of jungle grass.

"Come, old father of the forest!" shouted Tumbi, smacking the thick, loose, rough, dust-stained hide that stretched so incredibly over the huge frame of colossal bones. "Dost thou pretend the tree is too big to haul? Why, it is no bigger than the

105

stick thou tookst to scratch thyself with."

But Rajendra was not to be hurried. With a frond of bamboo poking from his mouth, he cocked a disdainful eye at Tumbi, as if to inquire what shrill insect was buzzing thus around him. In his own good time he began to haul again, on toward the distant forest track where the lorries would come to collect the timber. Now he stopped again, for a fallen jungle tree blocked his path. On either side were thick stands of trees which made a detour impossible.

"Undo the hauling chains!" ordered Kalyan and Tumbi quickly obeyed. The mahout lightly kicked the elephant, who knew precisely what was required of him. The fallen tree was held up by its branches, and Rajendra bashed at it with his forehead to get it moving. Again and again he thumped it lustily until it crashed over. Then Rajendra kicked it with a fore-foot and presently got it free from the tangle of other branches and bushes around it. Now he got his trunk round it, got his tusks under it and eased it away parallel to his path. With a huge crash he chucked it down, pushed it again with his foot, picked it up again and dumped it out of the way.

Now the hauling path was free for himself and for Pandit and Tilly who had begun to queue up away behind him. When they had hauled many logs to the track, they began to pile them up at the side, and sometimes Rajendra would help Tilly with hers.

"There is no elephant the like of mine," boasted Kalyan, during the noontide break, while the sun beat down fiercely, trying to penetrate the thick green mantle of the forest.

"How the earth would tremble if Rajendra and the Great King did battle together!" speculated Tumbi, his eyes gleaming with excitement at the thought of such an encounter. He squatted there, staring at Rajendra's gray, imposing presence. Would the Great King ever have submitted if he had been captured, wondered Tumbi. Would Rajendra perhaps have taken his place if he had remained free?

"Indeed, they are mighty folk, the elephants," agreed Kalyan, lazily, as he took one last satisfying draw on his *bidi*, the untidy tobacco leaf cigarette, tied with cotton, that he was smoking. "Bring Rajendra to me," he ordered Tumbi, who was only too pleased to obey.

Once again the dragging chains clanked, the giant feet plodded through the clearings. But Rajendra did not believe in working overtime, and when the sun began to throw long shadows through the jungle, he refused adamantly to haul a single log more. It was time for the evening bath and then supper.

While the bells jangled and the dust rose high,

107

Rajendra and the elephant gang tramped homeward. Alongside ran Tumbi, trying to fathom the wonder of how these gigantic creatures could so cheerfully toil in the service of men. It seemed to him that the power and strength and ferocity of the elephants was like a vast river flooding down irresistibly through the plains during the monsoon, until man came along and at a command the river grew smooth and placid, flowing gently among the fields and the pasture.

If the elephants belonged to the gods, then did men, too? Padding through the dust that coated his almost naked body, Tumbi glanced up at Rajendra. He glanced at the animal's great trunk, its huge feet. A blow from one, a kick from the other, or a thrust from those curving tusks, each could have killed him in the briefest of moments. Yet up there, riding high on the shambling shoulders, Kalyan could make that gray, time-grimed giant do his bidding without question.

Truly, there were many strange and wonderful things in life.

# 9

*The Great King's crime*

Meanwhile the Great King continued to terrorize the countryside round Kadanga, not so much by what he did as by his presence. Men said he was a rogue, but this was not so. He was old—his rough, stained skin was a palimpsest of many stories—maybe he had the fixed ideas of the old. And he needed food.

It was not easy to have a full belly, even at the best of times, if ever the times could be called best. Over the land people swarmed like ants, thousands of new hungry mouths came into being every day, and men were engaged in a desperate race for life. They hacked into the jungle, scratched at the earth with their wooden ploughs drawn by emaciated bullocks, sowed seeds, threshed the meager grain. Day after day they sweated under the towering sun to stifle the cry of hunger that arose from all the countless new mouths which had started to wail in the time it took for men to yoke their oxen and wade from one terraced, leechhaunted paddy field to another.

So the Great King's domain shrank every year, and now, as the dry season advanced, things became even more difficult. The bamboo wilted, the river grass grew dry and savorless. The dry famine winds burnt up the land. The Great King's belly rumbled with hunger.

The Great King with the young bull, his son, marched secretly again to the coffee estate where Tumbi had worked. They raided the planter's gardens, ate all his cabbages and helped themselves to the tree tomatoes. All this was done in such silence that no man knew they had been there until the morning. And in the morning, the young bull was still there . . .

"Master!" cried the houseboy, urgently, spilling the bed-tea as he rushed into the planter's bedroom. "There is an elephant on the estate road."

"Well, fetch the overseer," growled the planter,

smacking his lips distastefully as if he did not like the flavor of the morning; "tell Mr. Patel to deal with it."

"Master, I think elephant dying," said the houseboy, smart in his white turban and long white coat. "It is lying on side and groaning, very bad."

"The dickens he is!" The planter gulped down his tea and dressed hurriedly. He walked through the brilliant blue jacarandas that flanked the garden and down into the coffee. The houseboy and other servants pattered after him. Lower down the path a chattering group of coolies stood.

Fifty yards away lay the young bull. He had collapsed across a monsoon ditch and lay there heaving noisily. His trunk stretched out, his mouth gaping, his breath came painfully in great gasps and every now and then a terrible spasm shook his entire frame. It was clear that he was dying. Even the shrill voices of the coolies grew subdued as they watched.

Cautiously the planter walked closer to the young bull. He glanced around the neighboring coffee bushes and sniffed.

"It's obvious what's happened to him," he said to the topeed overseer who had joined him. "He's helped himself to a bag of sulphate of ammonia. Poor old devil."

That was what had happened. The young bull had come across some of the fertilizer put out ready

111

to be spread beneath the coffee bushes. He had enjoyed the acrid, salty flavor. Too late did he realize that it was not good.

"What will you do, sir?" asked the overseer. "Shoot it?"

"You know I can't do that," answered the planter, pushing back his bush hat and scratching his ivory white head. "If I do that without permission there'll be a row. I'll have to send a messenger to the forestry people."

While the young bull heaved out its life, the planter walked back to the bungalow. Before he had got as far as the veranda, he heard an agitated chorus of voices. For a moment he imagined the stricken elephant was trying to get to its feet, but then the houseboy came panting up the hill.

"Master! Big bull coming down the hill. Same one that smashed the watering cans!"

"What the blazes is he up to?" the planter speculated. He made his way farther up the estate road to a point where he could look straight down over the coffee. Meanwhile, the gang of coolies had hurriedly left the neighborhood of the young bull.

The Great King was making his way into the estate. If there was a fence it meant nothing to him. For a while the planter lost sight of him among the coffee and the shade trees, but before long the old elephant emerged in a clearing near some dry paddy fields and, crossing them, came onto the estate road.

He strode up to the young bull and snuffed him carefully all over with his questioning trunk. Inquiringly, tenderly, the massive trunk ran lightly over the heaving body. The young bull's ears flicked vaguely as if he knew the old bull was there, and he struggled fearfully to get to his feet. But the effort was too much for him, and he collapsed again with a loud and pitiful groan.

As if urging him to try again, the Great King trumpeted loudly, trunk in air. He was oblivious to the watching men, scarcely more than a stone's throw away. Now the planter suddenly noticed another big elephant making its way out of the distant jungle. It was a cow. She, too, strode through the estate, and the planter grimaced wryly as he saw her barging through the coffee bushes. She came the same way as the Great King, disappeared for a while, only to emerge near the road. Obviously several of the herd had been in the neighborhood during the night and were returning to help the stricken elephant.

Together the two grown elephants stood near the young bull, tramping here and there, touching him with their gentle trunks. But he was far gone, and his convulsions were painful to watch. However, he was comforted by the presence of his people, and

113

after he had been lying quite still for a while, he suddenly made one more effort to stand up. This time he was more successful. On trembling limbs, he heaved himself up and then, while the watching planter expected him to collapse once more, the Great King and the cow elephant, moving one on either side of him, supported his pain-racked body.

Slowly, patiently, the two great elephants helped

the sick bull along. Every now and then they paused, for the young bull's head hung very low and his feet would scarcely move. When next the convoy halted, it was for a long time. Immobile, that vast, gray group of elephants stood on the roadway, in almost contemptuous indifference to the men, who stared incredulously at what was going on.

But now even the urgings of the Great King

were of no avail. The young bull was exhausted by the effort. The poison was working virulently inside him. Gradually he sagged down between his two supporters. Yet they continued to stand there even after he had sunk down between their feet. For a while he sat there, his tusks digging into the roadway.

Another violent spasm shook him and then, with an agonized groan the men could clearly hear, he rolled over on his side against the sturdy legs of the Great King. The young bull was dead.

For a long time the Great King and the cow elephant stood there unmoving, as if they had not realized what had happened. At last the Great King snuffed the dead animal inquiringly and presently moved away along the road. Even then he did not depart. Restlessly he and the cow trudged up and down, occasionally trying to make the young bull move.

Sometimes they strode away a short distance, and the planter thought they were moving off. But each time they returned to keep vigil over the body that bulged awkwardly across the road.

"We'll have to do something about this," muttered the planter. "That young 'un has obviously handed in his chips. We shall have to report it and do something about disposing of the body. We'll either need a load or two of quicklime or a couple of hundred gallons of paraffin. Unless you eat elephant meat?" he teased the coolies.

"Oh, master!" the men answered, covering their faces in horror at such a suggestion.

"The men will not work while the other elephants are around, sir," the overseer said apologetically.

"Order them to drive the elephants off," the planter said. "I'll take the car and see the forestry people at Munjara."

At the bidding of the overseer, men fetched cattle horns and tin cans, just as they had the night the Great King amused himself with the watering cans. Without evident enthusiasm, the coolies advanced along the road, yelling and banging and blowing in a mounting crescendo of noise. There was much pushing from behind and some resistance from in front. Sweat glistened on brown bodies, and it was not only the sun that made them sweat.

The Great King ceased his parade and listened. But he was not impressed. He stood still and tucked his trunk into his mouth. At once the cattle horns stopped blaring and the drums stopped banging. In a scurry of dust, the coolies turned and fled. They knew what trunk-in-mouth meant. The Great King was going to charge.

When the planter saw what was happening, he

returned to the roadway armed with a double-bar-relled twelve-bore. The Great King had changed his mind and was once more standing immobile on the roadside. It seemed to the planter that in his poise, in the ponderous, dolorous set of his head, the whole despondent air of him, a pitiful grief was apparent.

All the same, the day's work had to be started, and the old elephant must be driven off. The cow

elephant had already started to move back to the jungle, scared by the strident noise. Followed by the emboldened coolies, the planter made his way cautiously along the road. The Great King watched him approach.

Fifty yards away, the planter fired his gun in the air, one barrel after another. The shattering roar echoed in the shade trees, startling the monkeys and the doves and the fruit bats. Quickly the planter reloaded, fired again high in the air, making a mental note that each time he loosed off a cartridge it cost him two rupees.

The Great King was striding off fast through a strip of cardamoms. This was a noise that thoroughly unnerved him. Again and again the roar of the shotgun echoed behind him, causing him to move faster each time. Away he strode, anxious now to get back to the jungle.

Eagerly the coolies set up their strident din once more. Knowing the elephant had been scared, they hastened to follow up their advantage. Hysterically the cattle horns blew, brazenly the drums beat, raucously human voices yelled in triumph, and the men forgot how they had fled a few minutes ago.

The estate was a riot of noise. Monkeys went leaping from bough to bough, chattering indignantly but keen to see what was going on. Glossy black drongos scolded harshly. The mynahs uttered their fussy call of *rahdyo rahdyo*. A hairy, cud-chewing water buffalo went crashing out of the bushes where he had been trespassing, moving faster than he had ever moved in all his life.

By now the Great King had vanished. For a while the men could hear him moving away into the distance. Then there was silence, broken only by the everlasting *tonk tonk tonk* of the coppersmith bird which seemed like the fevered pulsing of the earth under the mounting blows of the sun.

"Get the men to work," the planter ordered the overseer later on when the coolies mustered near the drying ground. As the gangs set out into the estate, they heard a sudden agitated voice crying out ahead of them.

From the direction of the jungle, a woman in a green sari came hurrying. Her arms were spread out, and she was shrieking loudly.

"An elephant! A great elephant!" she screamed. At that moment, the planter drove past on his way to visit the forestry authorities about the dead bull. When he saw the group of men clustered round the woman, he stopped the car and got out.

"What is it?" he demanded. "What is wrong with the woman?"

"She saw the elephant, master," someone ex-

120

plained. "She is afraid that she will be harmed."

"An elephant! A great elephant!" the woman started screaming again, a fleck of spittle at her lips. Her breast rose and fell violently, and her rolling, muddy eyes kept turning towards the jungle.

"It's all right," the planter assured her. "He has gone. He will not come back in a hurry."

The woman's nose stud flashed as she turned urgently towards the white man.

"*Dorai!* Master!" she cried, and her lips were blue. "He has killed my sister."

"What?" the planter echoed, disbelievingly. "Oh, my God!"

"We went out into the forest to gather firewood," the woman explained, a little calmer now. "Presently we heard much noise in the distance and then firing. We were afraid, for we guessed it was an elephant. We decided to come home, but on the way the great bull came towards us. He was upon us before we could do anything . . ."

"Yes! Go on?" the planter urged her tensely.

"I ran away. I was farther off," the woman said, plucking nervously at her sari. "But as I ran, I saw my sister stumble. Right in the path of the elephant. He hit her with his trunk. Only once. But it was a terrible blow. It rang in my ears like the breaking of a great branch."

121

"The elephant didn't attack you?"

"No, master, he marched straight on into the jungle."

"You are certain your sister is dead?"

"Yes, master. But I dared not stay. I ran straight down from the jungle."

"Whereabouts was this?" asked the planter. "Can you show us?"

At this the woman shrank back and put her hand to her mouth.

"All right," said the planter. He turned to some of the estate women who had silently joined the group. "Take her home and see she is looked after."

When they had led the wailing woman away, the planter set out towards the jungle, followed by the overseer and the coolies.

"We must find the body and make certain the other woman is dead," the planter said; though he had little doubt of that, he thought grimly. "You need not be afraid," he added to the coolies. "It is not likely that the old bull is still there or that he will return. He has probably had too big a scare."

But the Great King had returned. The men followed his tracks without much difficulty, but they could find no trace of the other woman. Nervously they called to each other to make certain the elephant was not lurking anywhere.

122

Then suddenly there was a cry from the overseer. He called the planter over to him and pointed.

"Look, sir, there is a woman's dress beneath the branches over there."

Wonderingly they made their way thither. It was so. Beneath a thick covering of branches and leaves and twigs and grass that had been plucked at random and strewn roughly over it, lay the body of the woman the Great King had killed.

That was indeed a strange thing. The Great King had returned to cover up the body of his victim. He had not intended to kill the woman. But he had been badly scared, and she had come in his path. It was as if he knew he had done wrong and wanted to conceal his crime.

For if the Great King had really meant to kill the woman he would have trampled her to a pulp, whereas there was little of violence about the look of the woman as she lay there in her disheveled blue sari.

# 10

*Evil spirit*

It happened that a little while after this, Rajendra became difficult, even unmanageable. Rajendra the gentle, the patient, the hard-working—Tumbi found it hard and sad to think of him as a ferocious, dangerous, chained-up monster of an animal, even though it was only temporary.

It started one day during the training of the seventeen-year-old bull which had been caught in Bapundi's trap a few weeks before. *Sinna dorai*, Little Master, as the mahouts had named this young bull, had already become fairly well-behaved. He had been put through his paces in the river, learned to obey elementary orders and occasionally went for a walk in charge of Rajendra, with the little cow elephant on the other side. None of these captives would be fully trained in this camp. Once they had become tractable, they would be sent to another training camp to complete their instruction. It would be several years before they could be put to work in a serious way.

The moment had come for *Sinna dorai* to be ridden for the first time. It was one thing becoming tame enough to take food from the hand of a man, quite another thing to allow that man to sit on your back. First, the young bull had to be lured into the teakwood stockade. This was comparatively easy, for he would do anything in return for a bribe of sweet jaggery. Tethered to Krishna, he was marched up to the cage while Rajendra ambled behind, ready to lend a hand if *Sinna dorai* suspected a trick.

The first sign that Rajendra was feeling irritable was when he gave the young bull a vicious shove from behind. Luckily he did not use his tusks, or Little Master might have been badly hurt.

"Take Rajendra away at once!" Ganesha Rao ordered sharply, but Kalyan had already acted promptly, for the old man could tell at a glance the difference between a playful barge and a vicious attack.

Once the young bull was in the teakwood cage, his attention was distracted by the tidbits he was given by Tumbi and some of the mahouts. Meanwhile, Gopal had climbed the side of the cage. The dry leaves of the roofing rustled as he got ready. From the center bar, which ran across the top of the stockade, a double pulley had been slung, with ropes attached. While four men took the weight, Gopal was lowered slowly down toward the unsuspecting young elephant.

*Sinna dorai* was too busy gobbling jaggery to realize what was happening until suddenly—lo!—a man was sitting on his back. He almost spat out the last lump of jaggery in his rage. He trumpeted shrilly and capered ponderously this way and that in his efforts to get rid of the man who squatted so insolently on his back.

It would have gone hard with Gopal but for the rope that held *Sinna dorai* to the bars of the cage. Even so, he bucked and kicked in a paroxysm of rage, while the dust churned up thickly, almost hiding Gopal from the onlookers outside.

"Haul up!" shouted Ganesha Rao, and Gopal was whisked into the air above the bull. For a while the young elephant sulked and would not accept any more food. Presently, however, he grew calmer; and at a suitable moment, Gopal came swinging slowly down again. Once more the young elephant was furious to find a man sitting on his back, kicking him behind the ears in an infuriating manner.

*Sinna dorai's* anger burst forth once more. The air rang with his trumpetings, he tried again and again to throw the man or crush him against the bars. If only he could dislodge the man, he would pound him to dust in a trice. But *Sinna dorai* did not know that this wretched, pestering man was safely attached to the pulley ropes that could whisk him out of the way in a moment.

For a long time the lesson proceeded while Tumbi and the others shouted encouragement and Gopal sweated. Slowly the elephant realized he was being mastered. For evermore he would be in the service of man. Already his spirit was but a shadow of what it had been the day he was brought from the jungle.

"He will make a good worker when he learns our ways," Ganesha Rao smiled, when the lesson was abandoned for the day. "In three years, he will be working full time."

Ganesha Rao made his way over to where Kalyan stood with Rajendra, whom he had made to sit. With his legs stretched out in front and behind, the

127

great elephant was sitting there placidly enough.

"Thou must watch him strictly," Ganesha Rao told Kalyan. "If he is coming on musth, there will be trouble."

"*Serri, iyer*," agreed Kalyan. "All right."

All creatures have their troubled moods from time to time, even men. With the elephants, it was the musth when, during the mating urge, they felt savage and wanted to commit violent acts. In their faces, just below their eyes, were the musth glands, and during this fevered period an unpleasant liquid trickled down from these glands into their mouths, making them more irritable than ever. Then the wildness of the jungle came over them, and they became uncontrollable.

All went well with Rajendra for a couple of days, but suddenly one evening, when the elephants were ambling back from their bath, he turned without provocation on Krishna. Tumbi and the camp attendants got out of the way quickly, and Tipane took Krishna away fast while Kalyan yelled and beat Rajendra over the head with a cudgel which he was carrying instead of ankus or goad. Near by Gokul stood ready with a spear which he had carried these last few days at Ganesha Rao's orders.

Krishna was wounded in the flank, a gruesome wound that would have been infinitely worse had not

128

the tips of Rajendra's tusks been sawed off. But worse
might come, and it was clear that Rajendra would
have to be chained up while the musth worked itself
out.

Tumbi watched anxiously to see if Rajendra
would obey Kalyan. While the other mahouts took
their mounts out of range of further trouble, Kalyan
made Rajendra march away from the camp to a clearing surrounded by bamboo trees near the side of the
long ravine. Here there was a special tethering stump,
where dangerous elephants had been chained before.

Quietly Gokul, Tumbi and the rest followed,
ready to chain Rajendra as soon as possible—and also
ready to bolt for safety if necessary. Almost passively
Rajendra allowed the padded chain to be fitted round
his leg; it was as if his spiteful mood had passed already. Kalyan made him sit while he got down, and
the elephant obeyed with only a slight hesitation.

But he stood up again at once, without waiting
for an order and suddenly, before anyone could so
much as utter a cry of warning, he had reached out
terribly at Kalyan and seized him in his trunk. With
a shriek the old mahout was lifted high in the air.
Aghast, Tumbi and Ganesha Rao and the other men
stood there helplessly, transfixed in their horror.

Next moment Rajendra hurled Kalyan away
from him as if the man had been a twig. Madly and

repeatedly the elephant trumpeted, raising his head on high and lifting his great forefoot as if he were doing a war dance. Now he felt his chains and strained mightily to break them. But the links had been well-forged by the smiths of Munjara, and the tree stump was well-founded in the deep earth, anchored by many tough roots.

Tumbi was the first to reach the stricken Kalyan.

Groaning feebly, the mahout lay spread-eagled fifteen yards away. He held a hand to his side, and it seemed that some of his ribs were broken. There was also a gash in his scalp. Already his *puggaree* was stained red.

While the trumpeting Rajendra raged behind them, trampling the earth and even gouging it with his tusks, the men gathered round Kalyan, each chattering this and that and offering shrill advice. But Ganesha Rao took charge and ordered them to fetch his assistant from the bungalow and to tell him to bring a *charpoy* or mattress with him in the jeep.

"Now, thou must keep still," he told Kalyan, whose usually brown face was the color of wood ash. "We do not know yet how badly thou art injured."

Expertly he ran his hands over the man's limbs, but these seemed undamaged except for various bruises and scratches where Kalyan had fallen. Soon the jeep came bouncing and swerving along the track, driven by Thimme Gowda, who had brought back the messengers and the *charpoy*, as well as a first-aid kit.

They staunched the blood that flowed from Kalyan's gray head, bound up the wound, and then carefully lifted the man on to the mattress. Slowly they carried their burden to the vehicle.

"He will have to be taken to the mission hospital," said Ganesha Rao. "I think some of his ribs are broken."

He gave Tipane, the second mahout, orders about feeding and watering Rajendra and also told him that Krishna must be caught as soon as possible so that he could examine his wound when he returned from the hospital. Then he and his assistant drove off with the injured Kalyan.

"This is a bad thing that has happened." Tumbi frowned to himself. He could scarcely believe what had occurred. In the space of a few terrible minutes, Rajendra had changed from a peaceable, plodding old friend into a raging, dangerous beast, eager to kill any who crossed his path.

There was much to be talked about that evening, as the men squatted in their huts and scooped the rice into their ready mouths. They talked of Krishna's wound and how the elephant had stood patiently while Ganesha Rao, standing on a platform of wood, had dressed it. They talked about other elephants that had run amok during the musth—in far worse a way than Rajendra. They talked, too, of the Great King, for news of the killing he had done had reached the camp.

Before night fell and the jackals began to wail, Tumbi went out to visit Rajendra and take him food. The elephant was busy ripping down what was left of the near-by bamboo branches. Sometimes he trod on one of them to force it down. He could just reach one of the trees if he shuffled sideways. The old bull seemed completely preoccupied in his meal, but Tumbi knew that all the time he was watching him.

"Why hast thou done this to Kalyan who was thy friend?" Tumbi asked, reproachfully, as he threw down the food he had brought. "Has an evil spirit taken possession of thee, old father?"

The great ears moved slowly forward, always a menacing sign in an elephant. Tumbi moved discreetly out of range. Rajendra leaned forward to the full extent of the short chain. The monstrous trunk went up, the gleaming tusks lunged out.

"May the poison soon leave thee," Tumbi said, gazing sadly at the gigantic animal. It grieved him to see him chained up thus, steadily growing more and more morose.

Tumbi had seen other elephants in musth. But somehow none seemed so terrible as Rajendra, whom he knew so well.

Out of his tiny eyes Rajendra stared back passively as he stuffed more bamboo leaves into his mouth with his expert trunk—that same trunk which had hurled Kalyan so viciously and which had at times in the past touched Tumbi affectionately on the shoulder. The elephant leaned forward again in the

133

hope of reaching the boy, though not this time with the idea of touching him affectionately. But he could not stretch the chain on his tethered hind leg, and it remained securely attached to the rocklike tree stump.

# 11

*The honey gatherers*

The trapping season was over; nor was much work being done in the camp. All day long the sun beat down more and more relentlessly. The long grass was sere and yellow; the fields were parched; the cattle lowed hungrily, and men looked anxiously at the sky.

One day Bapundi, the tracker, came to the camp. He was a brother of Tipane, the mahout, and together they decided to gather honeycombs from the nests of wild bees in the jungle. There were one or two good places not far from the camp, including a steep cliff face, festooned with creepers and little bushes, among which were several colonies of bees.

Tumbi and Gopal accompanied the brothers. They went towards evening, when the bees would be settling down after their labors. Even so, Tipane and Bapundi, clad only in their loincloths, took the precaution of smearing their bodies thickly with a paste of ash to deaden their scent and give them protection, while in addition Tumbi and Gopal would light fires at the foot of the cliff to bemuse the bees with the smoke.

There was also a nest in a fallen tree near the foot of the cliff. The basketmakers had told Tipane this, for they had been cutting bamboo near by. The dry grass clearing between the cliff and the bamboo jungle was strewn with signs of their work, for they had cut down many bullock cartloads of stems to take back to the village where they sliced the bamboo finely with razor-sharp knives and made matting for walls or little baskets for the coffee seedlings to be planted in. It was a long way for the basket makers to come, but there was good bamboo here, and they had a permit from the government to cut a certain amount.

Quickly Bapundi led the way through the long ravine to the cliff. They must work fast, for the light would soon go. Already the strident noises of the day were fading, and there was some relief from the stifling heat that choked the breath.

Other honey robbers knew of the colony of bees.

As the men padded through the yellow dry grass, high as their heads, they heard a rending sound ahead of them, a sound as of claws tearing rotten wood. Bapundi halted abruptly, the others in single file behind him. Tumbi, who was next to him, caught sight of a small brown figure scampering away through the grass. Next moment, from the fallen tree trunk, which was partly hidden by the grass, a much larger figure rose up. Shaggy and with a large white v-shaped mark on its chest, it was tall as a man and very much heavier. It was a sloth bear.

"Bear! Run!" cried Bapundi and everyone scattered, for the she-bear rushed out fiercely at them, while the little cub hopped up on her back and hung on tightly just behind her head. Tumbi ran fast, his bare feet thudding on the leaf-strewn ground. He did not know which way the men had run, nor did he care for the time being. All he was intent on was to get out of range of the sloth bear's terrible claws. More than one man in Munjara had a scarred face, some men were even blind, thanks to a sudden encounter with a sloth bear who, being deaf, was all the more dangerous. Other animals would have fled at the approach of men, but the she-bear was so intent on the honey she had raided that she did not perceive the intruders until they were almost on top of her.

Tumbi caught a glimpse of the sloth bear hump-

ing past, the cub clinging to her neck. As he made off in the opposite direction, he heard a scream from Gopal who fell headlong as the bear went past. Gopal went on screaming, and Bapundi came running back, armed with a cudgel and a knife. Tumbi followed him, fearful of what he would see.

The bear had vanished. Gopal lay grovelling in the undergrowth, yelling that the bear had clawed his face.

"Come, get to thy feet and let us tend thy wounds!" said Bapundi. "Thou art like a monkey fleeing from a panther."

"The she-bear has torn my face. I cannot see!" blubbered Gopal, holding his face in his hands.

"Why, thou has but been tickled by the thorn bush," jeered Tipane, approaching. "Take thy hands from thy face and thou wilt see well enough."

Somewhat shamefaced, Gopal peeped through his fingers at the men. It was true, there were only a few scratches on his nose and cheeks where he had fallen as he hurled himself out of the bear's way.

"Ask One-Eyed Kumar in the village," said Tumbi, "and he will tell thee the difference between thorns and a bear's claws."

"I tell thee, the she-bear struck at me as she passed," said Gopal, indignantly, wiping the sweat away with an arm. "Had I not been so agile, she

139

would surely have ripped me to shreds."

"But," he added hastily, "had I only been armed with a spear, I would have dealt with her."

"Assuredly," answered Tipane, drily, "thou wouldst now be wearing her skin to keep thee from the mosquitoes."

Warily the men approached the fallen tree again. There was no sign of the sloth bear, for she had taken herself off, anxious only for the safety of her cub. She had split open the trees and smashed up the bees' nest. The bees flew angrily around, but while the other men stood off at a distance Bapundi boldly collected what honeycomb he could. He seemed impervious to the bees, those few which were not repulsed by the coating of ash.

"We will eat the she-bear's supper," said Bapundi, gaily. He was a weird, devilish-looking figure, with his bright eyes gleaming from his camouflage.

Now the men gathered brushwood and bamboo debris that the basket makers had left and started two or three fires at the foot of the cliff. The fierce crackling made the monkeys chatter fearfully in the neighboring trees, but Tumbi and Gopal damped the fire down with moss, so that the flames subsided and great columns of smoke towered up instead.

Gopal glanced round nervously all the time they worked.

140

"Something is moving in the jungle," he muttered.

"Climb up the cliff with Bapundi and Tipane, then," Tumbi teased him. "Thou wilt be safe up there. Belike it is the she-bear come to look for thee and clasp thee to her in friendship."

With baskets slung on their naked backs, the two brothers climbed nimbly up the cliff, finding a toehold here, a fingerhold there. In the fading light and the wreathing smoke, Tumbi could scarcely make them out as they went in search of the clefts where the bees had their honeycombs.

By now the light had well-nigh gone, but a rich tropical moon had started to shine, as if some unseen hand had suddenly turned on its light. The fireflies were waving hectic patterns in the air. Somewhere a jungle crow was cawing restlessly, muttering like an old man under his breath. Farther away a muntjac deer barked uneasily.

"I tell thee, something moves in the jungle," Gopal said, licking his lips. His face shone like the moon itself.

"Come, tend thy fires," chided Tumbi, "else we shall get no honey for our pains."

Nevertheless, he, too, listened tensely to the jungle hush. The forest seemed to creep with furtive bodies. The heavy, scented air was charged with suspense. Menacingly the mosquitoes whined. The crickets chirped spasmodically. In a dried-up jungle pool, frogs croaked feebly, gasping for rain. On silent wings the nightjars glided among the trees or sat churring softly. From far off near the river, a fish owl uttered its booming cry. *"Bu bo, bu bo,"* called a horned owl; red eyes burnt somberly in the trees as the owl watched the men.

"Have they not found enough honey yet?" complained Gopal peevishly. "Surely their baskets are full by now?"

Along the cliff Bapundi worked nimbly, oblivious to the smoke and the bewildered bees alike. The moon picked out his naked body against the shaggy rock face. Tipane was making his way down. His bamboo basket oozed honey and was heavy on his shoulder.

Again the muntjac deer barked, this time more clearly. Something had alarmed it. *"Ba ha ha, ba ha ha!"* The deer barked, and something went crashing urgently through the undergrowth. Now a sudden rattling noise began to approach, and Gopal breathed heavily.

"It is only a porcupine," Tumbi assured him, "rattling his quills."

"The honey will need be sweet to make this night's work worthwhile," commented Gopal.

"Look not to taste thy share of it," Tumbi laughed, easing the fire so that it took fresh heart and gave off gouts of acrid smoke. "Bapundi will take it to the village and sell it to Lal, the bazaarman, who will sell it back to thee for ten times the price he gave."

"Listen!" whispered Gopal, hand to lips.

"I can hear naught but the thumping of thy cowardly heart," Tumbi whispered back.

"Thou cacklest like a jungle babbler," retorted Gopal. "Listen! Now, there again!"

Indeed, this time there was no doubt. From the neighborhood of the ravine came a coughing, rasping roar. It might have been the ugly sound of a badly set saw.

"Panther!" cried Gopal, and Tumbi knew he was right.

"Panther!" cried Gopal again, to the men on the cliff. All the jungle knew what was afoot. The red jungle fowl ceased scratching up the dead leaves. A spur fowl uttered its rattling cry. For a moment Gopal stood staring foolishly at Tumbi, the whites of his eyes gleaming in the moonlight. Then he ran away in panic across the grass clearing and into the trees.

The rasping cough was repeated, this time closer. Tumbi left the glowing fires and hesitated whether to follow Gopal or wait for Tipane and Bapundi. If he made up the fires, the panther would not come near them.

Then a horrifying scream echoed out from the direction in which Gopal had run. Tumbi stood rooted to the spot; Tipane joined him, panting from his hurried descent. A moment later Bapundi was at their side, grunting under the weight of the honey with which he was laden.

A series of screams and cries and groans startled them.

"The panther has taken him," Tumbi said, his mouth dry with fear.

"We must go to his aid," said Tipane, without great enthusiasm. Nervously they made their way into the jungle where they could hear something moving, but as they did so, they heard the panther roar again. This time he was farther off and in the opposite direction.

"He could not roar if he had taken Gopal," Bapundi pointed out logically. They began to call Gopal by name, and he answered in a moaning voice. They found him not far away, ruefully examining the calf of his leg as he squatted on the ground in the brilliant moonlight. In his flight from the panther, he had blundered upon the porcupine, who had left several barbed quills in his leg.

144

"We must cut the quills out," said the practical Bapundi, dumping his load; "else they will fester and thy flesh turn rotten."

Poor Gopal groaned at the prospect. He had not enjoyed his honey gathering.

# 12

*Panic*

It was during the noontide rest the following day that one of the mahouts remarked that there was smoke on the air.

"It is the sawyers who are burning their leavings," someone suggested.

"It is the cattlemen on Munjara hill who are burning the old grass," said someone else.

"Nay, this smoke comes from the jungleside," Tipane observed, thoughtfully sniffing the air. That was true, for the wind had changed during the morning. A fresh, welcome breeze was blowing, bringing hope of the rains that would assuage the terrible thirst that now racked the land. The leaves had wilted, the soil had cracked in long fissures, the drinking pools were little more than liquid mud.

As the breeze strengthened, so did the smoke become more noticeable. Tumbi saw that one or two of the elephants lifted their trunks uneasily to sample the air. Tipane stood sniffing the wind. He chewed his betel nut quid doubtfully.

"There is fire in the jungle," he said.

"Look!" cried Tumbi, pointing upward. Through the trees a troop of black-faced monkeys went swinging urgently, chattering as they passed. Several green parakeets flitted overhead, flying downwind in the same direction. Many insects boomed through the trees.

Tipane stood on one leg. He was beginning to be alarmed for he did not like the signs at all. He guessed only too well what had happened. Because of that stupid Gopal, the smoke-fires had been forgotten. They had probably smouldered all night, and then the rising wind had fanned them into life. The jungle floor was littered with tinder dry rubble, while the long grass in the ravine would blaze up at a spark.

Now Tipane was in charge of the camp. Kalyan

was in the hospital. Thimme Gowda was shivering with malaria. Ganesha Rao had had to visit the police superintendent for a consultation about the Great King now that the death of the woman had been reported.

Tipane felt guilty because he had allowed the camp to spend a lazy morning by the river. Now while he debated whether to send the men out to try

and douse the fire before it became too great, Gokul
came loping out of the jungle from the direction of
the ravine.

"There is much fire in the jungle!" he cried. "It
is moving this way fast."

"Is it too big to beat out?"

"Hai! Man!" Gokul raised a hand expressively.
"It burns everything. The grass in the big *nullah* is

alight, and the bamboos all round are on fire. Nothing can halt it. I had to run fast, or it would have roasted my back."

He laved his sweating arms and face with water from one of the hollowed-out tree trunks that were used as drinking troughs for the elephants.

A jungle fire moves with terrifying speed once it takes hold. The dry grass and the feathery bamboos would act like torches fanned by the wind. As if Gokul's words had conjured it up, the fire became suddenly apparent. In the distance could be heard the crackling of flames; smoke belched down the ravine as if from a funnel.

It was possible that the camp itself would be safe, for the entire space of it was composed of flat bare earth on which not a blade of grass grew, while the huge deciduous trees might remain unscathed. But the surrounding bamboo jungle and the wide swath of grass came too close to be comfortable, and Tipane decided that the elephants must be taken to a place of safety.

Tilly and Pandit had gone off into the jungle some time before. Fortunately they had not gone far in the noontide heat and were soon located by their mahouts. The biggest problem was Krishna, who was still suffering from his wound, which was stubborn to heal, and the four young captive elephants. Two of them, the young cow and *Sinna dorai*, were now tame enough to be led away at once with Krishna, but the two latest captives were still caged.

They had to be shackled first while the front bars of the teakwood stockades were raised and Tilly and Pandit were maneuvered into position. The young captives squealed and struggled in their fear, infected by the men's urgency. All the elephants were restive, for they knew the fire was approaching. Gopal fumbled about in one of the cages and was knocked sideways against the bars by the young elephant he was trying to rope.

"Take thyself away, thou useless one, thou son of an owl!" shouted Tipane from Tilly's back, as the miserable Gopal limped away, hugging his bruised ribs while the bandage round his torn leg trailed on the ground. "Pass up that rope to Gokul, Tumbi, thou."

Tumbi leapt to obey, and the young elephant was at last secured fore and aft with padded chains round two of its legs and a soft rope halter round its neck. Ponderously, awkwardly, the convoy moved off through the jungle with a great clanging of bells and crashing of undergrowth. Tumbi and the unmounted attendants ran alongside through the dust, urging the young elephants on, while Tilly and Pandit strode on solemnly. Ahead of them, Govindra

151

on Krishna cried out to ask what Tipane intended to do.

"We must cross the river," Tipane shouted back. "It will be safe there near the mangrove swamp."

The elephants were striding out fast now, and Tumbi fell behind. He glanced over his shoulder and wondered how far the fire had reached. A mongoose went scuttling suddenly across his path, and a sambar hind bounded away through the trees in the distance.

All at once Tumbi thought he heard an elephant trumpet away beyond the camp. With a gasp of dismay, he came to a halt.

"Rajendra!" he shouted to the disappearing mahouts. "We have forgotten the bull."

He was dumbstruck at the realization that they had done so. Only in blind panic could they have forgotten Rajendra.

He shouted again and Gopal turned inquiringly for a moment but then hurried on again, and in the jangle of bells and the thud of gigantic feet and the jabbering of men, nobody else heard Tumbi's cry. All were too anxious to flee from the fiery terror behind them.

"Gopal! Thou art a son of a jackal!" Tumbi fumed, but to no avail. His bare chest rose and fell as he stood there irresolute. He was terrified of the fire and, now that Tipane and all the rest had disappeared, he felt terrifyingly alone. His eyes grew wide with fear as he caught sight of flames rising above the tops of the trees. Moreover, how would Rajendra behave if he went back to him?

Then he heard Rajendra roar. Tumbi's mind was made up. He could not abandon the old bull to such a fate. He might die in the flames, but assuredly he would die of sorrow and shame if he did not go to the help of Rajendra. Tumbi ran back through the trees, and a gust of acrid smoke met him. Already he could feel the wind hot with the dragon breath of the advancing fire. The parched branches and shriveled fronds and creepers popped and spluttered like fireworks.

Tumbi ran back panting through the deserted camp. One of the huts had caught fire from floating sparks, and the bamboo thatch went up in a sudden belch of fire. Now he could see the fire itself. The grass and the lantana bushes in the ravine were roaring up in one long torch of flame.

Now he could feel the heat on his naked limbs. The smoke made it painful to breathe. Quickly he unwrapped his *dhoti*, so that he was clad only in his loincloth, soaked the *dhoti* in the water of one of the drinking troughs and draped it over his head.

Rajendra was chained up a hundred yards from the camp, that much nearer the line of the fire. His

153

hind leg was stretched out painfully as he strained at the chain. With his trunk he slashed frenziedly at the wreck of the nearby bamboo.

Cautiously Tumbi approached the elephant. Rajendra seemed vaster than ever as he towered there over the boy, his trunk snaking here and there as if seeking a way out of danger.

It was not only from the heat of the raging fire that Tumbi broke into a sweat as he stood there. He knew that, in his terror, the elephant might turn on him and obliterate him in one fearful blow.

"Now, old father," Tumbi croaked, for his mouth was parched unbearably, "I have come to aid thee."

In response the elephant trumpeted loudly and tore down a branch which he immediately flung from him vehemently.

Trembling, Tumbi approached Rajendra. Placing his hands together briefly in front of his face, he muttered a prayer to all the gods of the forest, even to the elephant gods, to protect him. With sweat pouring down his glistening body, he picked up a stone and searched for the peg that held Rajendra's chain. He hit his knuckles painfully so that the blood flowed, but he scarcely noticed this. Sobbing with frustration, he tried to wield the stone, but it was too cumbersome. He flung it down and, racing back to the camp, returned with a mallet he had found.

Above him the great gray leg, the massive, gray, wrinkled body loomed, yet already it seemed that Rajendra was calmer. Tumbi's confidence grew. He had always had faith in the old bull. Now the musth had gone from him, and he must surely realize that Tumbi was trying to help him.

Nearer through the bamboos and grass scrub, the wall of flame was advancing. Fiercer than the eye of any tiger, the flames glared redly. Down the funnel of the ravine, the fire rippled on like a molten tide.

Again Rajendra trumpeted, as if urging the boy to hurry. The ponderous feet, with their great toes, moved to and fro, and Tumbi got ready to leap aside if necessary.

Then at last, with a cry of relief, Tumbi felt the iron bolt give. The chain fell apart. Rajendra was free.

"Now, go thy fastest, old father," cried Tumbi, hoarsely, drawing the wet *dhoti* round his head again, for showers of sparks were being flung down on the scorching wind. "Save thyself."

But instead of at once taking advantage of his freedom, the elephant wheeled round towards the boy. Tumbi's heart stood still as he crouched there, dwarfed by the colossal body. Was the poison of the musth still working? Was the elephant maddened

155

with fear? Tumbi had no time to think. Next moment the elephant's trunk had stretched out and, seizing Tumbi by the waist, lifted him high in the air.

Tumbi seemed to be sailing through the tree tops. He tried to scream, but no sound passed his lips. He was certain his last hour had come. It was on this very spot that Kalyan had been flung down, brutally injured, ten days ago. The elephant would fling him down from on high and then trample him to pulp in his frenzy of terror and rage.

But no such thing happened. Instead, Tumbi, dazed by this sudden devastating turn of events, found himself set firmly but gently on Rajendra's back, just behind the huge, domed, wise head and enormous ears. He came to his senses and, sobbing in thankfulness and wonder, seated himself more securely astride, with his heels close in behind the animal's ears.

"Rajendra knows! Rajendra knows!" he cried in triumph. He was right to have had faith in the old bull.

Away through the camp, where several huts were now blazing, Rajendra strode mightily and swiftly, his immense shoulders heaving up and down, one leg limping somewhat from the chain. On into the jungle on the far side, he strode downwind towards the river, while behind him the fire raged at the creepers and the yellow grass and the many-stemmed bamboos which spurted weird feathers of flame.

# 13

*Judgment but not justice*

Now the Great King's fate was sealed. He had wrought great havoc in the countryside around Munjara. He had ruined many acres of crops, stripped many plantain groves of their fruit. He had damaged a godown, wrecked a dwelling house. He had pursued a man in a bullock cart and had even attacked a temple elephant. He had smashed up a boat on one of the tanks. He had pulled up many white signposts so that they had to be replaced with black ones. He had terrorized the peasants for miles around, and complaints about his behavior were frequent.

Above all, he had killed a human being.

Vainly did Ganesha Rao plead that the Great King was not a rogue, that the killing had not been intentional, that the feeding grounds of the elephants were being encroached on every year, forcing them to seek food where they could. It was no use. The Great King was condemned to death.

Lestrange, the famous *shikari*, was asked to shoot him. Lestrange could have filled the Ark with the creatures he had shot. From the tiny mouse deer to the great swamp deer, from the civet cat to the flame striped tiger, he had shown many times that man, armed of course with a gun, was superior to any of his fellow mammals. Lestrange's bungalow was a morgue of heads and pelts. The wastepaper basket by his desk was made of an elephant's foot. The door-stop was an elephant's tooth.

Lestrange was appointed the Great King's executioner.

As if he had heard news of the fate men had ordained for him, the Great King had disappeared for some time after this. But this was not surprising, for he traveled many miles in search of food. Nothing was heard of him and Lestrange became impatient, for the monsoon was about to break, and he wanted to carry out his task before the countryside became impassable and nothing could be accomplished.

Then it was reported that a big elephant had been seen in the hills beyond Munjara. Lestrange went by car along the dirt road as far as he could, taking Bapundi with him as his tracker. Lestrange's houseboy was a cousin to Tumbi, who wheedled him into persuading his master to take the boy with them, on the understanding that he helped with the work of the camp. Bapundi, too, told Lestrange that Tumbi was a good tracker.

A cattle herdsman told them how he had seen the Great King. He showed them the elephant's tracks. Bapundi measured them carefully with grass, and there was no doubt about their identity. The Great King was there, up in the little downland hills which were covered with scrub jungle.

Tumbi was sad at the thought that the Great King must die. He was a little frightened, too. He glanced at Lestrange: he must be a bold man indeed to contemplate such a deed so nonchalantly.

The following day Bapundi came down to Lestrange's camp with the news that the Great King had been feeding on a strip of grassland beyond the scrub which ran almost to the top of the hill. A herd of gaur was grazing in the same neighborhood, and these might make it more difficult to approach within range of the old elephant. There was only one side from which to approach, as the other side of the hill fell away in an almost sheer precipice overlooking a wooded valley, past which the dirt road from Kadanga ran.

"We shall have to try, whatever the wind," decided Lestrange, looking at the leaden sky. "If he gets our scent, he will have to come down the hill to get away. If he does not, then we are all right."

Armed with a high-velocity rifle, Lestrange set out with Bapundi and Tumbi. Through thick scrub of lantana bushes, they made their way, while spur fowl cried fussily around them, and a magnificent peacock with trailing tail went slinking away.

"*May-awe! May-awe!*" the peacock caterwauled.

Far up above the hill, a bird wheeled patiently. It was a white-backed vulture. Tumbi glanced again at Lestrange. Did the vulture know the white man was coming and that where he went there would be death?

Carefully Bapundi read the tracks and read the wind.

"We go this way, master," he said presently, turning at right angles through the scrub. "*Katta pothu* grazing higher up. They warn elephant if we go too close."

By "*katta pothu*," Bapundi meant the gaur. Si-

lently now, the men crept up through the scrub. They could hear the herd feeding not far away, and in a little while they caught sight of the lookout bull, standing guard. High as a tall man, the bull was glossy black, with a powerful shoulder ridge and neat white stockings.

Lestrange eyed him in admiration, but the bull was safe from his gun, for a shot now would have alarmed the Great King.

Beyond the lookout bull, the herd grazed, dark brown cows, golden calves, other black bulls. They came and went among the sere grass and the thickest lantana bushes. All around were their tracks, and Tumbi stared at them in astonishment at their size.

The lookout bull was restless. Muzzle raised, he quested the air, moved to and fro. The herd caught something of his suspicions and ceased their grazing. The golden brown calves huddled at their mothers' sides. The bulls moved forward menacingly.

Bapundi, too, anxiously tested the air. Crouching behind a bush, he lifted his chin to beckon Lestrange on. The air of the hill was treacherous. It eddied here and there and could not be depended on.

Lestrange slipped off the safety catch. He did not want to have to shoot, but if the herd charged, he might be forced to do so. Though one shot among a trampling herd of angry gaur would not help much.

Stealthily the men moved on, trying to get out of the wind that had aroused the herd's suspicions.

"Elephant yonder, master," whispered Bapundi, and Lestrange caught a glimpse of giant ears flapping in the distance above the scrub. Evidently the Great King did not suspect anything yet, for he was busy tearing down a branch. Maybe the gaur had followed him to browse on the leaves he conveniently broke down and left.

Now the men could see all the herd, twenty gaur. They had gathered closely together and were staring into the bushes where the men had been a moment ago. Great heads tossed as the handsome beasts read the messages the fickle wind brought them.

Suddenly, as if at a signal, the entire herd began to move. Down the slope they moved, cows and bulls and calves, a compact mass of powerful bodies. The earth shook, dust rose, bushes rustled and crashed.

There was no time for concealment. For their very lives, Lestrange and Bapundi fled out of range of the thundering herd. Tumbi flung himself into the shelter of an impenetrable bush and with thumping heart watched the pounding hooves churn past him on both sides, while the dust from the herd's passing choked his mouth and spattered his eyes.

Four score hooves went galloping by, and the earth trembled. Downhill the gaur went, and the peacocks caterwauled in agitation.

Now the Great King had taken alarm. When the men came together again, dust-stained and shaken, they saw that the old elephant had ceased his feeding. He had moved off several yards and now stood with ears fanning speculatively and trunk up-curved.

Lestrange edged across the hill. He expected the old bull to make his way downhill and wanted to make certain of a suitable traverse shot. If he reached a certain clump of lantana he had in view, he would be bound to have a clear view of the elephant.

But, contrary to Lestrange's expectations, the Great King did not come downhill. Instead, he strode off slowly toward the open grassland near the summit, where the jagged skyline fell away hundreds of feet below.

"What's he trying to do?" the white man muttered. "Is he trying to work round behind us . . ."

Tensely he crept on, oblivious to scratches and insects alike. For a while he could not see the elephant and had to make his way in what he guessed to be the right direction. Nor could he hear the Great King, for the old elephant was either moving off with all the astonishing silence of which he was capable

or he was waiting somewhere trying to locate the exact whereabouts of the man before charging.

Telling Bapundi and Tumbi to remain where they were, Lestrange went on alone, every nerve tingling. At any moment a monstrous shape might come striding at him, as ready to kill as Lestrange himself was.

Up in the cloud-ridged sky, the vulture wheeled with a grace it never possessed when on the ground. In the lantana bushes, a shrike called harshly and incessantly. Then it grew suddenly silent and went skulking away as if abashed by the tension that had settled on the hill.

For a long time Lestrange waited behind the scrub before emerging into the open, flat on his belly in the grass. Seventy yards away the Great King stood. Lestrange wrapped the rifle sling round his arm, settled down with icy calmness. He would get a chest shot, take the old bull in the heart. But now the Great King swung round so that he was sideways on to the man.

"Brain shot," Lestrange thought, automatically. "Through the ear." From the side a heart shot was impossible, for the immense shoulder blade would be in the way.

Before Lestrange could fire, the Great King turned again and walked off slowly up the hill. For the time being a shot was impossible, and Lestrange watched eagerly to see which way the elephant would go. Evidently he had lost the scent trace of the men, for up here on the brow of the hill the breeze was blowing more strongly from the precipice, bluffing up over the edge and making the grass ripple.

Knowing this, Lestrange followed, though carefully. Frowning in response to the question going through his mind, he watched the elephant ambling along close to the sheer edge of the hill. Now the Great King paused, as if in contemplation, and Lestrange realized this was his chance. Though the animal was alarmingly close to the edge, he must risk a shot, for if it once disappeared into the surrounding scrub that partly lined the rim of the hill, he might not get another opportunity.

The hem of the cloud rack had now lifted somewhat, and the Great King was silhouetted against the sky, the lower part of which burned in all the blood-red, ominous glare of the sunset. There was no sound on the hill. Not a bird cried, even the insects seemed to be still. The wind had ceased to breathe. Hunter though he was, Lestrange himself breathed more quickly at the imposing sight of the huge elephant standing there, motionless, majestic, mysterious in all the grandeur of his size and innate power. As the man watched, a tiny, brilliant bee eater, scarcely as long as a man's hand, darted into a bush, perched there a moment, flashing its many colors and then vanished, swift as a flash of light.

In that brief moment as he saw all this, Lestrange was almost stunned by the realization that the same power that had fashioned that diminutive bird had also created the gigantic elephant he now confronted. His heart sank as he thought of the impending death of this animal that had lived a man's span of years in the jungle and must now die only because there seemed to be not enough room on the earth for both the wild animals and man, who gathered everything to himself and was never content.

But Lestrange was a hunter. He had come to do a job. Once again he settled down with steady nerves to sight his rifle on the target, as he had done a hundred times, five hundred times before. Muntjac or tiger, crocodile or elephant, Lestrange never missed.

With an eye hard and unfeeling as a diamond, he sighted on the elephant. Through the ear drum to the brain. So simple. The roar of a high-velocity cartridge and the immense body would sag to the ground as useless as a dirty cloth.

But then, even as he eased the pressure on the trigger, a strange thing happened.

Before he fired—and how many times afterwards he was to emphasize this—before he fired, the elephant

170

moved. For a moment it seemed as if the Great King was going to turn downhill after all. Instead, moving his head slightly in the man's direction, he turned the other way, toward the precipice. With a glowing aura from the sunset around him, he seemed to slide rather than walk toward the edge. A trick of the light? A trick of the eyes? As Lestrange, elbows on ground, braced himself for the crash of the shot, the Great King vanished.

A split second later, the rifle roared out. But it was afterwards. Lestrange was adamant about that. He fired after the Great King fell. A hundred times in the club he told the story and was never shaken from what he said. He fired after the elephant disappeared.

It was as if the Great King knew that he must die, but preferred to die in his own way. In Munjara men still talk of the death of the Great King.

# 14

*Farewell, Great King*

One day, several months later, Tumbi came along the dirt road from Munjara, riding on Rajendra. Behind them swung the other elephants, Tilly and Krishna and Pandit and Naga, ridden by Tipane and the rest of the mahouts. The camp at Munjara was being closed, and the elephants were going to work at another place.

Kalyan had never really recovered from his accident. He was left with a limp, and his confidence was gone. He was old, too, and Ganesha Rao said he could

172

no longer be a mahout, though he still worked with the elephants. It was taken for granted that Tumbi should now be accepted as a full mahout, which was what he had longed for all his life. Besides, he was the only person old Rajendra would now tolerate as a rider, and at eighteen Tumbi knew more about elephants than most men.

So, proudly, he had taken the cracked bell from Rajendra's neck and hung his own bell, the brass bell his father had left him, in its place. The new bell rang out sweetly, and no other bell possessed the same tone. Well satisfied, Tumbi now sat high up there on the mighty back, his heels behind the elephant's ears, surveying the land as they passed sedately along. The green rains of the monsoon had replenished the earth. The granaries were full. The jungle trees were aflame with color. The nim trees put forth their tiny stars. The flame-of-the-forest burned brilliantly. The tulip trees were hung with crumpled, crimson bells.

As Rajendra strode along the undulating dirt road, Tumbi glanced up at the towering precipice from which the Great King had fallen to his death. He shuddered at the thought of the elephant crashing hundreds of feet into the ravine.

Was the Great King truly dead or did his spirit perhaps still wander through the jungle? His body had never been found, except by the circling vultures and the mewing kites and the jackals that laughed and screamed in the night like tormented souls. They gave him honorable burial as he lay in the deeply wooded ravine. The termites helped. Even the porcupines came and gnawed through the huge tusks. The Great King had lived a full life, and now he lay at rest in the jungle where he had once roamed freely.

Yet indeed his spirit did survive, even if it was only in the memory of men who would go on talking about him for many years to come, so that a legend grew up about him. Tumbi would remember him, too, and now as he rode along on Rajendra, he looked down into the dark ravine where the lorikeets called and flitted.

"*Salaam*, Great King!" he said, raising a hand in salute. As he spoke, Rajendra, too, lifted his trunk and trumpeted in *salaam*, as he had always been trained to do. One after another, the other elephants followed suit. Their trunks went up, they trumpeted a *salaam* and strode gravely on, with a plodding of stately feet and a ringing of bells.

Was it merely that they had heard Tumbi's salute and had taken it for a command? Or did they perhaps, in their mysterious, unfathomable way, know that their brother, the Great King, lay there in the jungle from which they had all once come.

F